The Time Devil
Teaching & Drama Script

Francis Gilbert

Copyright © 2017 Francis Gilbert
FGI Publishing, London UK, **sir@francisgilbert.co.uk**
All rights reserved. This book contains material protected under International and Federal Copyright Laws and Treaties. Any unauthorized reprint or use of the original material written by Francis Gilbert is prohibited: these sections of the book may not be reproduced or transmitted in any form or by any means, electronic or mechanical, including photocopying, recording, or by any information storage and retrieval system without express written permission from the author / publisher. Although based on 'real' people, all the characters in the script are fictional and the script does not intend to represent 'reality'.
ISBN: 154671300X
ISBN-13: 978-1546713005

DEDICATION

To Favor, Misha, Miski, Nicola, Padraig, Tai, Miss Prescott & the National Maritime Museum.

ACKNOWLEDGMENTS

Thanks, as ever, to the staff at the National Maritime Museum who assisted in any way they could.
Thanks to all the Goldsmiths staff and students who helped out, especially Connie Freire De Souza, Harriet Salisbury, Alice Spacey-Meaghan. Harriet was particularly helpful by reading the script so carefully.
Thanks to all the teachers and students at Deptford Green too.

Contents

CHARACTERS 6
INTRODUCTION 7
ASSESSING YOUR READING SKILLS 8
    SKIMMING AND SCANNING 8
    SUMMARISING 8
    CLARIFYING AND QUESTIONING 9
    PREDICTING 10
    COLLABORATING 10
    LEARNING TO LEARN 11
    BECOMING A MINDFUL LEARNER 12
        Learning intentions 13
        Becoming a mindful reader 17
        Free Mapping and Writing 19

THE LEARNING JOURNAL 20
    YOUR BOOKLET 21

GOLDEN RULES 21

LESSON 1 22
    Mindful reading meditation 22
    Learning intentions 22
    Learning script 23
    SCENE 1: WALKING TO DEPTFORD GREEN SCHOOL: FORDHAM PARK 28
    Learning script 36
    Learning Activities 41
    Assessment point 42
    Independent study 42

LESSON 2 44
    Mindful reading meditation 44
    Learning intentions 44
    Learning script 45
    SCENE 2: MEETING THE TIME DEVIL 46
    Learning Activities 48
    Assessment point 49
    Independent study 50

LESSON 3 .... **51**
   Mindful reading meditation 51
   Learning intentions: skimming and scanning 51
   Learning script 57
  SCENE 3 CHARLIE: PRINCE FREDERICK'S BARGE, APRIL 1736 58
   Learning Activities 63
   Assessment point 64
   Independent study 64

LESSON 4 .... **66**
   Mindful reading meditation 66
   Learning intentions: questioning 66
   Warm-up 1: asking questions about your thoughts and feelings 67
   Warm-up 2: Asking questions about your reading 68
  SCENE 4 TAI: BATTLE OF TRAFALGAR, 1805 68
   Learning Activities 74
   Assessment point 75
   Independent study 75

LESSON 5 .... **76**
   Mindful reading meditation 76
   Learning intentions: summarizing 77
   Activate Prior Knowledge 78
  SCENE 5 PADRAIG: THE GREAT COMET 1843 78
   Learning Activities 84
   Assessment point 85
   Independent study 85

LESSON 6 .... **86**
   Mindful reading meditation 86
   Activate Prior Knowledge 86
   Learning intentions: predicting, filling in the gaps 87
   Making Predictions 88
  SCENE 6 NICOLA: THE 2ND OPIUM WAR: 1856 88
   Learning Activities 94
   Assessment point 96
   Independent study 97

LESSON 7 .... **98**
   Mindful reading meditation 98
   Learning intentions: collaborating 98
   Learning script 99
  SCENE 7 FAVOR: BENIN CITY: 1897 100

    Learning Activities *105*
    Assessment point *106*
    Independent study *107*

LESSON 8 .... **108**
    Mindful reading meditation *108*
    Learning intentions: learning to learn *108*
    Learning script *109*
  SCENE 8 MISKI: FEMALE SOLDIER, GERMAN SHIP, 1914-18, WWI WARSHIP, JUTLAND
.... 109
    Learning Activities *114*
    Assessment point *115*
    Independent study *116*

LESSON 9 .... **116**
    Mindful reading meditation *116*
    Learning intentions: summarizing part II *117*
  SCENE 9 THE GREENWICH MERIDIAN: THE FINAL CONFRONTATION 118

END OF THE TIME DEVIL SCRIPT **128**
    Learning Activities *128*
    Assessment point *130*
    Independent study *130*
    Utopias and Dystopias *130*
    The 'Time-Travel' project *131*

LESSON 10 .... **132**
    Learning intentions: motivating yourself *132*
    Learning script *133*

FINAL ASSESSMENT POINT **133**
  MOTIVATION 133
  SKIMMING AND SCANNING 134
  SUMMARISING 134
  CLARIFYING AND QUESTIONING 135
  PREDICTING 135
  COLLABORATING 136
  LEARNING TO LEARN 137
  INDEPENDENT AND COLLABORATIVE STUDY BASED ON THE WHOLE SCRIPT 137

THE KEY QUESTIONS FOR RECIPROCAL READING **139**

ABOUT THE AUTHOR **140**

Characters

CHARLIE (based on Misha): a Key Stage 3 Deptford Green student

FAVOR: a Key Stage 3 Deptford Green student

MISKI: a Key Stage 3 Deptford Green student

NICOLA: a Key Stage 3 Deptford Green student

PADRAIG: a Key Stage 3 Deptford Green student

TAI: a Key Stage 3 Deptford Green student

Various historical and contemporary characters based on the exhibits & staff in the National Maritime Museum; all entirely fictional, and not intended to represent reality in any way.

Teaching script roles: TEACHER, QUESTOINER, ASSESSOR, MOTIVATOR, SUMMARIZER, LEARNING TO LEARN CHIEF.

The Time Devil: Teaching & Drama Script

Introduction

This script was written to help secondary students' reading at Key Stage 3 (KS3 = 11-14 years). It was created with the help of many people, most especially the six Deptford Green students who agreed to be the main characters: Favor, Misha (renamed as Charlie in the script), Miski, Nicola, Padraig and Tai. It should be noted, that they have given their permission to be named and written about in an entirely fictional way in the following story. Working with the wonderful staff at the National Maritime Museum (NMM), Connie Freire De Souza, Harriet Salisbury, Alice Spacey-Meaghan and Ms. Vikki Prescott, the students' English teacher at Deptford Green, I listened to what everyone said about the museum and their ideas for plot-lines which might interest KS3 students. I then asked the six students to pick six objects of interest to them from the NMM collection. After they'd done that and we'd discussed how these objects might be used to formulate an engaging narrative, I went away, thought long and hard, and then wrote the script, listening to constructive criticism from all the aforementioned people. They had to read many drafts; I like to thank all of them for the patient, constructive way they gave me comments. This really helped me write a better script. The previous year, I carried out a similar project with Deptford Green but did not collaborate in the same way; I can see that the collaboration has made me write a much more incisive script than the previous one.

I have framed the drama with a 'teaching script' which aims to teach KS3 students various reading skills, but most particularly Reciprocal Reading (or Reciprocal Teaching as it is sometimes know).

The script is a work in progress; one of the advantages of publishing it through a Print on Demand (PoD) platform is that corrections can be quickly made and the book republished. If you do have any suggestions, or you spot any mistakes, please email me (see below).

I would like it noted that although I have worked with the above institutions, this is purely my own work and I take full responsibility for the content and/or any errors etc.

Francis Gilbert: **sir@francisgilbert.co.uk**

Assessing your Reading Skills

Before reading this book, you're going to have a go at assessing your reading skills so that you and your teaching have a "benchmark" as to what you feel your skills are; at the end, you will complete the same survey to see if you have improved.

Skimming and scanning

In general, when you read texts in school, how good do you believe you are at skimming (quickly looking through a text and working out what it means) and scanning (quickly looking through a text to find a specific piece of information) through texts and working out what might be happening in them? Please tick:

4	3	2	1
Not very good	OK	Good	Outstanding

In general, when you read texts outside school, how good do you believe you are at skimming and scanning through texts and working out what might be happening in them? Please tick:

4	3	2	1
Not very good	OK	Good	Outstanding

Please write a comment about how you good you feel you are at skimming and scanning:

Summarising

In general, when you read texts in school, how good do you believe you are summarizing the content of what you read?

Please tick:

4	3	2	1
Not very good	OK	Good	Outstanding

In general, when you read texts outside school (which can include social media/articles you like etc), how good do you believe you are summarizing the content of what you read?

4	3	2	1
Not very good	OK	Good	Outstanding

In general, when you read texts in school, how good do you believe you are summarizing your understanding of what you read? Please tick:

4	3	2	1
Not very good	OK	Good	Outstanding

Please write a comment about how you good you feel you are at summarizing:

Clarifying and questioning

In general, when you read texts in school, how good do you feel about asking questions which might help you work out what a difficult text means? Please tick:

4	3	2	1
Not very good	OK	Good	Outstanding

In general, when you read texts outside school (which can include social media/articles you like etc), how good do you think you are at asking questions which might help you work out what a difficult text means?

4	3	2	1
Not very good	OK	Good	Outstanding

Please write a comment about how you good you feel you are at clarifying (working out what difficult texts mean by yourself) and questioning:

Predicting

In general, when you read texts in school, how effective are you at predicting what might happen next? Please tick:

4	3	2	1
Not very good	OK	Good	Outstanding

In general, when you read texts outside school (which can include social media/articles you like etc), how effective do you think you are at predicting what might happen next?

4	3	2	1
Not very good	OK	Good	Outstanding

Please write a comment about how you good you feel you are at making predictions of what might happen next in a text:

Collaborating

In general, how good do you think you are at collaborating with other students in school so that you might improve your learning about a topic? Please tick:

4	3	2	1
Not very good	OK	Good	Outstanding

In general, how good do you think you are at collaborating with other students outside school so that you might improve your learning about a topic? Please tick:

4	3	2	1
Not very good	OK	Good	Outstanding

Please write a comment about how you good you feel you are at collaborating:

Learning to learn

In general, how good do you think you are at working out what helps you learn more independently:

4	3	2	1
Not very good	OK	Good	Outstanding

Please write a comment about how you good you feel you are at learning about your learning:

Assessing yourself based on this review

Add up your scores!

Mostly 1s and 2

If you are mostly scoring 1s and 2s for this assessment, you are probably a strong, confident reader who should find this script quite easy to read, but may need some practice in order to read it with expression. You should be stretching yourself by doing the Independent Study questions and reading. You should see "pictures" of what is happening in your mind like watching a film. You should also be "modelling" good reading and collaborating with other people in your group: you should be helping people who are struggling to read, you should be showing them how to read with expression, you should be asking questions easily and fluently that really help people think more deeply about the script, you should be able to take notes quite easily, and do the writing tasks without struggling to understand them.

Your reading intentions should include: learning to summarize expertly by explaining the script to other people, learning to improve your questioning by really asking questions that help other people understand the script.

Mostly 2s and 3s

You will be able to read this script, but you might find parts of it difficult. You may find that you become distracted at times because you do not immediately "see pictures" of what is happening in your mind. You will need to make an effort to be motivated to read the script all the way through. You will need to discuss elements of the script with your colleagues and need to encourage yourself and other people so that they enjoy the script.

Learning Intentions: to build your confidence and enjoyment in reading by discussing the script with other people, to practice reading in a group and learn to read with expression.

Mostly 3s and 4s

You may well find elements of this script quite difficult. You may find it difficult to be confident and motivated regarding your reading. You will need to work with at least someone who is scoring 1s and 2s in your group if there is someone available. You may well need input from your "real" TEACHER or a Teaching Assistant to help you. You will need to find ways to get motivated to read; you should try to find connections with the script and things that interest you in your life.

Learning Intentions: to build your confidence and enjoyment in reading by discussing the script with other people, to practice reading in a group and learn to read with expression.

Becoming a Mindful Learner

It is very helpful to be mindful about your learning; to realize that we learn every second of every day we are alive in some way or another. Learning is not just limited to the classroom or the text book.

Mindfulness can mean a great many things but one simple definition is:

"Paying attention in a particular way: on purpose, in the present moment, and non-judgmentally." Jon Kabat-Zinn
("Mindfulness | ACT Mindfully | Acceptance & Commitment Therapy Training with Russ Harris")

As we said when talking about learning intentions, there are three components to mindfulness which are very helpful when you are setting your own learning intentions:

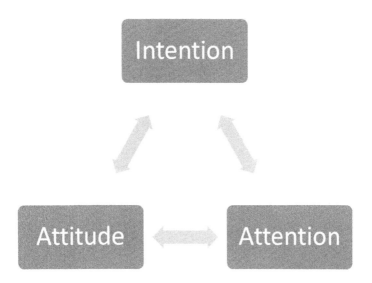

You will see from the diagram that intentions comes first. Every lesson (and outside lessons if you can) we want you to set clear learning intentions for yourself by considering two very important things: attitude and attention.

Let's show you how it works. For every lesson, you are in, you could make these learning intentions:

> I intend to have a positive attitude towards my learning.
>
> I intend to pay attention to what the teacher says and doing the things that help me learn.

Learning intentions

We are getting you to think hard about your "learning intentions" while reading this script; we like the word "intentions" rather than "goals" or "objectives" because we want you to think hard about what you intend to learn before you complete each lesson.

The two vital elements linked to your intention to learn are your attitudes towards your learning and the quality of your attention when you learn.

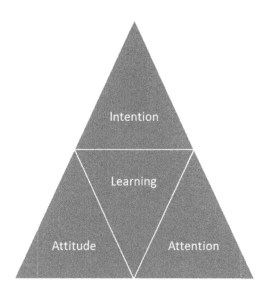

The above diagram shows that to learn you need to have the "intention" to learn, and the right attitudes and attention so that you can learn effectively.

The Learning Intention you could have for every lesson

On the most basic level, every lesson you learn will have this fundamental learning intention, which could be written as: "I intend to learn more about myself and the world I live in by having a positive attitude about what I am learning and paying close attention to the things I am supposed to learn about." So, if you're ever stuck about what learning intention to set, use this one!

The overall intentions of this script are to help you improve your reading skills, to learn how to read more difficult texts by yourself, to learn how to appreciate and enjoy museums and cultural artefacts, to learn how to collaborate well.

Learning Charm

In order for you to personalize your learning, we'd like you to find a special object or charm that could symbolize your learning and help keep your focus upon your learning. Choose an object which you have with you and try to figure out through discussion why this object symbolises your learning. For example, you could have your home key, get it out, look at it, feel it, and explain why it embodies your learning intention talking about why the object suggests the right attitudes and attention; "This key symbolises my learning intention because I want to unlock the door to reading in a better and more enjoyable way; this key is my learning charm because it symbolises the happiness of going home and if

I am to learn well I should have a happy attitude. This key is also very focused upon opening my front door, and I want to have that kind of focus when I pay attention in lessons."

Task: find a learning charm that symbolises your learning intentions for this unit of work, and symbolises the right kind of attitudes and attention that you want to have. Write a poem about the learning charm and why it symbolises positivity and attention for you.

How?

The next step is to consider you might gain a positive attitude and develop focused attention in lessons. To be positive, you may want to adopt a "Growth Mindset" and believe that you can do things if put in the effort. You might want to sit next to someone who helps you learn best etc.

To pay attention to the things that help you learn, you might want to consider trying to making connections between the things you like and your learning, so that you are motivated to learn. You might consider taking regular breaks so that you maintain your concentration.

What?

Then you need to think of things that will show you have achieved your learning intentions.

E.g. if you are positive in your approach, you will probably have read what you are required to read and a bit extra, and if you are paying attention, you may well achieve good results in your assessment at the end of the unit.

Setting Learning Intentions

Now set some overall Learning Intentions for yourself using this script to help you.

Learning intention	How? (Process)	What? (Product)	Learning Charm?
I intend to improve my confidence in reading aloud.	By reading aloud with a positive attitude and reading passages every lesson, and every lesson.	Dramatic reading of the script at the end of the unit.	E.g. the buttons on my blazer because they are shiny and always happy.
I intend to improve my ability to summarize what I have read.	To give regular spoken summaries of what I have read in my group, and to write regular summaries in my learning journal.	Spoken summaries; written summaries	E.g. my right hand because it is good at squeezing some objects into smaller sizes.
I intend to improve my ability to skim and scan texts.	To learn the skills of skimming and scanning.	To show I can pick out key quotes and read texts quickly by summarizing them.	E.g. my legs because they can run fast past lots of things very quickly.
I intend to improve my ability to collaborate in a group.	To learn how to be positive in my group, smile at people, celebrate my and other people's successes.	To accomplish all the group tasks: complete the group reading of the script by the end of the unit.	E.g. my pencil case because it holds lots of different things like a group should hold lots of different opinions.
I intend to	To regularly	To have a list of	

improve my ability to ask questions which help my understanding of what I have read.	ask questions which help people understand.	good questions in my learning journal which help me understand the script.	
I intend to improve my concentration when I am reading.	To regularly pay attention to my reading taking a positive attitude towards it.	Completion of the script, and reading of other texts related to the script.	

Becoming a mindful reader

Mindfulness is about developing these three things:
- Your intentions
- Your attention
- Your attitudes

One way to improve your reading skills is to become a "mindful reader".

If you improve your ability to pay attention, you will improve your ability to read. This is why developing your mindfulness skills will also help you improve your reading skills.

You may have done some mindfulness activities in school already; it is sometimes used in school to help both TEACHERs and students deal with stress. It can also help people concentrate.

We are going to do a short mindfulness activity now and then get you to think about applying your mindfulness skills to your reading.

The Three-Step Mindfulness Meditation

OK, let's go: adopt a relaxed but not slumped position in your chair, bringing your back away from the chair and sitting up straight in a relaxed way. Now shut or lower your eyes, putting away all distracting things (definitely phones!) and just take a minute to see how you are feeling in your body and your mind. What feelings are in your legs, your arms, your chest, your throat, your head?

Now, take a few minutes and concentrate upon your breath, follow your breath as you breathe in, and follow it in your mind as your breath out. If necessary, say:

- **I AM BREATHING IN (AS YOU BREATHE IN)**
- **I AM BREATHING OUT (AS YOU BREATHE OUT)**

Variations on this might be:

- **I AM BREATHING IN AND CALMING MYSELF**
- **I AM BREATHING OUT AND SMILING**

Or:

- **EACH IN-BREATH IS A NEW BEGINNING**
- **EACH OUT-BREATH IS A LETTING-GO**

Don't worry if you become distracted by thoughts, feelings, just accept them as they are, and then return to concentrating upon the breath. The whole point of the mindfulness practice is to learn to bring your attention back to your focus. This is why it is so helpful for developing reading skills because once you get used to returning back to the focus of your breath, you will also learn to return to other things you have to focus upon such as reading difficult texts.

Once you have done this for two or three minutes, now imagine that your breath is going through your whole body, that your in-breath is soothing and calming your throat, your chest, your arms, your legs and going right down to your feet. And then as you breath out, imagine the breath soothing and calming like a warm bath your body as it rises through your feet, your legs, your abdomen, your chest, your throat and head.

Take a moment to notice the sensations in your body: how are you feeling in your stomach, in your legs, arms, feet, the surface of the skin…

Now open your eyes. Could you before, you read a passage, make sure that you do a short mindful reading meditation (see below).

This is what is called a **"3 step mindfulness"** meditation. To recap it involves these 3 things:

1. Becoming aware of your thoughts, feelings and sensations in your body (about 30 seconds)
2. Concentrating upon your breathing in and breathing out, and if distracted by thoughts/feelings returning to concentrating upon the breath by saying in your head "breathing in, breathing out", or "In…Out".
3. Expanding your awareness to become aware of the sensations in your body.

Please do a mindful reading meditation at the beginning of each lesson

Before you start a lesson in this book, I'd like you to do a short mindful reading meditation.

To do this you must do these 3 things:

1. Discuss what you intend to learn during the lesson (look at the learning intentions at the beginning of each lesson to help you with this).
2. Do a short mindfulness "3 step meditation" meditation like the one above.
3. Do some free "mapping" or writing about anything that is on your mind, with a focus upon what you have learnt about reading, and what you want to learn more about. See Free Mapping and Writing section for more on this.

Free Mapping and Writing

After you have finished your mindful reading meditation, I'd like you to have a go at doing some "free writing or mapping" for a three minutes.

What is "free mapping or writing"?

Free writing is writing whatever you want in your learning journal; the only rule is that you have to keep writing for the specified length of time: 3 minutes. You could copy out your name, you could write the football scores, you could write about thoughts and feelings, you could summarize what you learnt last lesson, you could write a poem about your cat, your mum, you can write what you want. No one else will see this piece of writing.

To make the exercise a bit easier for students who do not like "writing", they could have a go at doing some "mapping": writing words and drawing around them. This could be a spider diagram. A word and a picture. The only rule is that you keep pen to paper and you write at least three words. For example:

What's the point? Reasons for doing this…

1. You learn that writing can set you "free".
2. You learn to write "automatically".
3. You get more practice in writing and mapping.
4. You can let out any feelings.
5. You have time to yourself with a pen and paper.
6. The evidence is that having a go at free writing regularly helps you write more formally because you get practice in writing.
7. It encourages "flow" with writing: you get into the practice of writing quickly and fluently.
8. You don't see writing as a chore, but as a joy.

The Learning Journal

You are going to put all your findings – your free writing, your notes, your independent study work -- in a Learning Journal. You will be asked to map out of your ideas on A4 sheets of paper which you must date/number as appropriate.

Your booklet

You will put your best work together into a booklet to present to the class at the end of the project.

Golden Rules

- Everyone is a teacher: this means you need to be ready to explain points to other people, show other students "best practice", ask good questions which draw people out and get them enjoying their learning. It does not mean that you threaten them with detentions; you are aiming to be kind, caring teacher who uses positive encouragement rather than threats. Only the "real" teacher can impose sanctions. You all must teach each other in the way a kind, caring teacher would.
- Be kind to yourself and other people: wish yourself well and other people.
- Be mindful of yourself and others. Find joy in working together with other people: it is a very special thing to read with other people.
- Smile and keep smiling! Fake it until you make it! Be happy!
- Always help each other: smile at each other, congratulate each other when you've tried.
- Avoid criticizing each other: do not say "You're stupid" "You're dumb" "Stop mucking around" etc. Instead set a good example and patiently get on with your work and guiding people BY EXAMPLE rather than CRITICISM.
- Be polite: say hello and goodbye with real care and attention.
- Be disciplined about working together; make sure you keep focus at all times and don't talk about things which are nothing to do with the lesson.
- Swap roles! Make sure that everyone has a go at reading different roles.
- Learn to talk freely in the different "teaching script" roles; learn to talk like a Teacher, Assessor, Motivator, Learning to Learn Chief, Questioner, Summarizer. Powerful learners are all of these roles 'rolled' into one!

Lesson 1

Mindful reading meditation

Before starting your reading for the lesson, make sure you do a short mindfulness meditation to help develop your ability to set some clear reading intentions, to pay attention and adopt a positive attitude. Please see the section **Becoming a Mindful Reader** if you have forgotten how to do this.

Learning intentions

Learning intentions	Learning Charm	How?	What?
I intend to learn more about Reciprocal Teaching/Reading.		By reading the lesson carefully with a positive attitude, by following the instructions, by asking if I don't understand; by having a go at it and reviewing what I have learnt	Discussion work; written notes.
I intend to learn about different group roles.		By following instructions by paying close attention, discussing points I don't understand, asking questions, making notes.	Discussion work; notes; answering the questions/tasks set.
I intend to learn more about how collaboration helps you learn.		By reading the script about this point, and discussing it with members of my	Discussion; notes; answering the set tasks.

| | | group with a positive attitude and paying close attention to what people say. | |

Are there any other things you intend to learn about? Please discuss and/or note them down...

Learning script

TEACHER: I don't like reading.

QUESTIONER: Hey, aren't you supposed to be a teacher? Aren't all teachers supposed to like reading?

MOTIVATOR: Good point, Questioner, as the Motivator in the group, I have to say that telling your students that you don't like reading is a bit demotivating!

ASSESSOR: And as the Assessor, I would have to grade that teaching strategy as unsatisfactory. I don't think any school inspector would be happy to hear a teacher say that!

LEARNING TO LEARN CHIEF: As Learning to Learn Chief (L2LC), I think we need to give the teacher a break: my job, which is being in charge of Learning to Learn is about helping people improve their learning by thinking about their learning and what works for them and what doesn't. My first question is: what do we exactly mean by a teacher and what is expected of them?

SUMMARIZER: As Summarizer, I would have to sum up the meaning of being a teacher as someone who helps other people learn.

TEACHER: And it's true, I have a problem. I mean I am actually a school student who has been asked to be a teacher in a group. And I don't feel comfortable with the role at all! First of all, I don't really read that much!

QUESTIONER: Why are you not comfortable being a teacher? I don't get it.

MOTIVATOR: Come on, Teacher, everyone likes you in the group so you don't need to be frightened.

ASSESSOR: And having seen you outside lessons, I have seen you read the sports' news on your news on your phone, and all that Snapchat, Facebook, Twitter stuff all the time. You're always reading!

SUMMARIZER: So, to sum up, are we saying that our teacher is a much better reader than they think?

LEARNING TO LEARN CHIEF: And perhaps we think reading means reading in school when reading is a lot more than that.

TEACHER: Hey thanks guys, you're cheering me up. I didn't enjoy the thought of being a teacher, but I can see now that I have helped you learn a bit because we've all thought harder about what teaching and reading is.

QUESTIONER: What is the point of making students teachers anyway? I mean, we have got a real teacher over there, aren't they supposed to teach us?

MOTIVATOR: But I reckon I learn more when another student teaches me something: I kind of listen more carefully. I'm less scared somehow and this makes me relax and listen more carefully.

ASSESSOR: And when you become the teacher you quickly realize what you know and don't know because you have to explain it in our own words.

SUMMARIZER: So perhaps the teacher is the person who learns the most in the classroom because they are always trying to explain things.

LEARNING TO LEARN CHIEF: This is interesting. It's at this point, I would like to give us all a new term to learn. This term is called 'reciprocity' as a noun, and 'reciprocal' as an adjective.

TEACHER: Can you all write the heading 'Reciprocity' in your learning journals. What do you think it means?

QUESTIONER: Aren't you supposed to tell us? Isn't that why you're a teacher?

MOTIVATOR: Hey, it's better if we look up words for ourselves and learn to learn things for ourselves.

ASSESSOR: So let's look it up in the dictionary – or on our phones. Here look, Google says:

noun: reciprocity

the practice of exchanging things with others for mutual benefit, especially privileges granted by one country or organization to another.

QUESTIONER: What does that mean?

SUMMARIZER: Let's try and put it into our own words. Hmmnnn.

LEARNING TO LEARN CHIEF: It kind of means "you get what you give".

TEACHER: Yes, it's when you give something, you expect to get something of equal value back.

QUESTIONER: So, if I help you with your reading, I expect you to help me when I find some passage difficult to understand.

MOTIVATOR: Or if I am really positive about your abilities, then I expect you to be nice about me.

ASSESSOR: Kind of. It's more than people being nice to each other though, it is about people valuing each other, really valuing what they have to say.

LEARNING TO LEARN CHIEF: OK, let's all write down in our learning journals our definitions in our own words about what reciprocity means.

(Everyone should do this)

TEACHER: And I think we're ready now to introduce the next idea: Reciprocal Reading.

QUESTIONER: Is this when everyone helps each other with their reading?

MOTIVATOR: Hey, Questioner, well done! You've got it in one. It's about really trying with your reading, and then expecting the other people in the group to try as well.

ASSESSOR: It's also about us all assessing our reading skills and figuring out how we might improve our reading together. The reciprocity comes in because we assess ourselves and assess each other, valuing each other's contributions.

LEARNING TO LEARN CHIEF: And to add to that, let's see what dear old Google says:

Reciprocal teaching is a reading technique which is thought to promote students' reading comprehension. A reciprocal approach provides students with four specific reading strategies that are actively and consciously used to support comprehension: Summarizing, Clarifying, Questioning, Predicting and Evaluating.

QUESTIONER: what does that all mean?

TEACHER: We're going to find that our now!

MOTIVATOR: We're all going to read an exciting, brilliant play which about some students at Deptford Green school who get tricked by a nasty devil. And we're going to use Reciprocal Reading to read it together and question what it is about.

ASSESSOR: The first thing we're going to do is have the teacher say what parts we are going to read: Charlie, Tai, Padraig, Miski, Nicola or Favor. They are all real students who have given their permission for their names to be used for this crazy play.

SUMMARIZER: And when the group has finished reading the scene, each person is going to do answer these questions with all of us helping each other to talk in detail about the play.

LEARNING TO LEARN CHIEF:

The key questions for Reciprocal Reading

SUMMARIZER:

First part of the reciprocal reading cycle

What is this scene about? What is happening in it? How might I best summarize my overall understanding of the passage: do I have a unsatisfactory, satisfactory, good or outstanding understanding of the passage? (Summarizing)

Second part of the reciprocal reading cycle

Are there any difficult bits we don't understand? Is anything not very clear? If so, can other people in the group help us understand the scene better? (Clarifying)

QUESTIONER:

Third part of the reciprocal reading cycle

Does anyone have any questions to ask about the passage? Do you have any questions about how you might improve your understanding of the passage? E.g. Do (Questioning)

LEARNING TO LEARN CHIEF:

Fourth part of the reciprocal reading cycle

What does everyone think might happen next? Is there anything that is NOT said in the scene/passage that we think might be important to consider? (Predicting/hypothesizing)

ASSESSOR:

Fifth part of the reciprocal reading cycle

How well are we reading? What could we do to improve our reading? (Assessing/Evaluating/learning to learn)

TEACHER: Then the cycle begins again with the next scene. At that point, the goal is that the role of the Teacher passes on to another person so that everyone has a go at being the Teacher. The idea is that you do the cycle a few times and then it becomes "natural" and you naturally ask the right questions that come to mind. You "internalize" how to read well by summarizing your understanding of the passage, by clarifying difficult bits, by asking good questions that make you think more deeply about the text, and by predicting what might happen next.

QUESTIONER: I am confused. What am I supposed to be doing? Can someone help me?

MOTIVATOR: Don't worry, we'll have a go with the first scene and then you'll begin to get the idea.

ASSESSOR: It generally takes a few lessons before people get the hang of Reciprocal Reading – sometimes called Reciprocal Teaching. It always starts with people being confused because it's quite complicated.

SUMMARIZER: But to sum up, it really is about people learning to read together and discuss what they are reading.

LEARNING TO LEARN CHIEF: That's a good summary, SUMMARIZER. OK, let's all write down in our learning journals, what we think Reciprocal Reading means.

TEACHER: And now, let's have a go at doing some Reciprocal Reading of the first scene of the play. There is one important point to add; the dialogue in the script contains what are called "asides": these are moments when the speaker tells us what he/she is seeing and experiencing at that moment or wants to narrate some aspect of the story. Shakespeare and many playwrights use "asides" a great deal to describe action which otherwise can't be conveyed in dialogue. You will need to express the "asides" in a different tone of voice, as though you are speaking to someone telling a story, rather than just engaging in a conversation. Try experimenting with the way you say them and all the dialogue so that you say it in a clear and expressive way.

Scene 1: Walking to Deptford Green school: Fordham Park

NICOLA: [aside] Me, Favor, Tai and Padraig met up in Fordham Park just before school. It was a nice summer's morning, a bit overcast, but the air was cool.

TAI: Hey, I think we're going to do some meditation first thing in school today! It's all part of these new lessons to help us deal with stress!

FAVOR: Yeah, I found it a bit strange last time I did it; shutting my eyes, concentrating upon my breathing and wishing people well!

CHARLIE: A bit weird, but still I found it quite relaxing.

TAI: I don't like imagining everyone watching me with my eyes closed.

NICOLA: Me neither, although when I pay attention to my breathing for a bit, it does calm me down.

PADRAIG: I think it's a bit of a waste of time to be honest, but hey, it's a change from normal lessons.

TAI: Yeah, I'm quite looking forward to it; it's only for a few minutes and it kind of relaxes you…

[aside] we all would have been feeling nice about things except that there was this big black bird flying above us.

NICOLA: What's that big black bird flying up there doing?

FAVOR: That's a big bird!

NICOLA: It's a bit bizarre, it keeps circling over us!

PADRAIG: It'll probably do its business on our heads!

TAI: Yeah, we should move.

FAVOR: Let's go up on New Cross Road and sit under the bus shelter – Miski and Charlie said that they'd meet me there when I spoke to them yesterday. And going there will mean we can get away from that bird! It's really creeping me out!

NICOLA: Yes, Miski and Charlie said they'd meet me there as well. [aside] So, we all walked up the hill to the bus stop.

PADRAIG: Hey TAI, did you get that message from Charlie and Miski last night?

TAI: Yeah, something about downloading some TimeBook app. I downloaded it, but it didn't do anything!

FAVOR: I call BS. I mean, like you can download an app that can make you travel through time! Every scientist like me knows that it's impossible.

PADRAIG: But did you download it? I did!

TAI: I think you did Favor!

FAVOR: So maybe I did, but it hasn't done anything. It's just sitting there clogging up memory on my phone. I think I'm gonna delete before we go to school, it'll ruin my phone.

NICOLA: I downloaded it too, but I don't think it's doing any harm. It looks kind of pretty!

TAI: Yeah FAVOR, don't delete the app just yet! Charlie and Miski told us to sit here at the bus stop at eight thirty just before school, and they texted me last night to say that they wanted to show me something to do with the TimeBook app.

PADRAIG: [aside] We would have stayed at the bus stop but the bird had followed us there! It had landed on the roof of the bus shelter and then bent its head down so that it was looking straight at us.

NICOLA: Ahh! I hate that bird looking at me! It's so ugly!

TAI: Oh, come on! Let's go back towards school. I don't think Charlie and Miski are going to show up and I don't want to be late! But I'm not frightened of a bird!

FAVOR: [aside] So, we all walked back towards school, leaving the bus shelter, trying not to be freaked out by the bird, but as we walked along, we all heard this strange whizzing in the air above us.

PADRAIG: [aside] We looked up and saw the bird again!

NICOLA: What the hell is that bird doing? It's definitely following us!

PADRAIG: [aside] Then suddenly there was a massive explosion and it felt like we'd been blown off our feet!

TAI: [aside] But it was strange because we were still walking down New Cross Road, but we were seeing things as we did, our eyes were all fuzzy from the explosion.

NICOLA: [aside] We were in a daze.

FAVOR: It feels like all the buildings around us have been destroyed!

PADRAIG: And I can hear screaming, and sirens, and an air raid warning.

TAI: It's crazy, what is going on?

NICOLA: [aside] Then as suddenly as the explosion happened, everything was gone and we were walking down New Cross Road again and the traffic was screeching and beeping around us.

PADRAIG: [aside] Like it normally does.

NICOLA: Hey, did you hear that?

FAVOR: Yeah, a huge explosion.

TAI: And screaming and sirens!

PADRAIG: And now it's like nothing happened.

NICOLA: And thank goodness, that horrible black bird has gone!

TAI: [aside] We walked back down the hill to Fordham Park and could see the students going into Deptford Green school

NICOLA: Well, Charlie and Miski weren't at the bus stop, and they're not here, and I can't see them going into school. They're not going to show up. They haven't even texted us.

PADRAIG: Oh, hang on a minute, Charlie's calling me…Charlie?

CHARLIE on the phone: Hey, something mad is happening down here. You've got to get down to Deptford Bridge DLR station. Right now!

PADRAIG: CHARLIE… Are you there? He cut me off! The line is dead.

TAI: MISKI is calling me now… Miski, is that you?

MISKI: TAI, you've got to help us. Something's going wrong. Deptford Bridge DLR station has gone. There's a river, a deep river, and we're with lots of guys dressed in funny clothes. Old really smelly clothes. It stinks! It looks like some kind of army is approaching!

TAI: MISKI? I got cut off. What's going on?

NICOLA: And my phone's getting kind of warm. And the app, my TimeBook app is doing something. It's glowing, swirling.

FAVOR: Mine is too!

TAI: And me.

NICOLA: This is not an ordinary app. And look, that bird is back!

PADRAIG: Wait, do you think the TimeBook app and that bird are somehow connected?

NICOLA: Do you think the TimeBook app can make you travel back in time like Dr Who's Tardis?

TAI: I'm beginning to wonder…Maybe Miski and Charlie are somehow trapped in another time zone?

FAVOR: I don't want to think about it! Let's run! Charlie and Miski need our help!

TAI: I feel like that bird is giving us evils!

FAVOR: Look, there's bound to be a good, rational explanation for the bird; we're not in a horror movie! This is real life!

NICOLA: Let's get down to Deptford Bridge DLR station and see if we can find Charlie and Miski.

PADRAIG: But what about school?

NICOLA: Miski and Charlie are in trouble. They sounded like they needed our help.

FAVOR: Maybe we should call someone, or tell the school?

TAI: And tell them that they downloaded a time-travelling app and it's done something weird to them?

NICOLA: Maybe Charlie and Miski are trapped in another time zone?

FAVOR: That's ridiculous, Nicola. You have such a wild imagination.

TAI: Yeah Nicola, even if it were true, do you think our teachers are gonna believe that?

NICOLA: Well, MISKI told me last night on WhatsApp that she was hoping that the TimeBook app would help her time-travel.

FAVOR: Why didn't you tell us this before?

NICOLA: I don't know. I felt a bit embarrassed for Miski, I suppose. It sounded so stupid!

TAI: If this is a prank, I'm gonna kill Charlie and Miski!

FAVOR: It's just like them to prank us…

TAI: Look, it's only short walk through Margaret McMillan Park. We can go down there, have a look and then we'll probably be back in time for the first lesson. We'll just say there was an accident or something.

NICOLA: Which is kind of true.

FAVOR: Hey, wait for me!

PADRAIG: Where are we going?

TAI: Come on, let's speed up, that bird is still following us.

PADRAIG: Where are we??

NICOLA: Hey, you noticed something funny around here?

TAI: There are kind of strange noises.

FAVOR: And lots of smoke!

NICOLA: And this does not look like a park anymore, more like a factory or something.

TAI: But now it's gone.

FAVOR: And now it's back to normal. Yes, the Albany Theatre is right here, and all the market guys are selling all their cheap tacky rubbish!

NICOLA: Don't call it that, it's merchandise!

TAI: Stop arguing you two, we need to get down to the station quickly.

PADRAIG: Especially since that bird is still following us!

FAVOR: [aside] And we turned the corner, went underneath an archway, and suddenly found ourselves not in Deptford at all, but in the countryside. The city had completely and utterly gone.

NICOLA: [aside] We were in a large field which was separated by a big river.

TAI: Hey look, I can see Charlie and Miski! They are with a bunch of very dirty looking people!

PADRAIG: They're just people with funny clothing!

TAI: And some nasty looking weapons!

NICOLA: [aside] Charlie and Miski were walking with a big gang of people dressed in dirty smocks who were carrying axes and knives.

TAI: Charlie! Miski!

CHARLIE: Hey Tai, Favor, Nicola! Whatever you do, don't lose your phones!

MISKI: Charlie lost his, and mine's run out of battery!

FAVOR: What is going on?

TAI: [aside] A large army of men on horses were galloping towards the dirty people holding axes. Right behind them was a man wearing a crown on his head.

KING (FAVOR): I am your King and I command all of you to give up your weapons and surrender!

PEASANT 1 (CHARLIE): Not until you stop making us pay taxes which we can't afford!

KING (FAVOR): If you don't surrender, I will kill every last one of you.

PEASANT 2 (MISKI): Never!

KING (FAVOR): Then soldiers of the crown I command you to charge!

NICOLA: [aside] And it was terrible to watch. The dirty peasants had no chance. The soldiers rushed at them on their horses and stabbed them with their lances and slashed at them with their big silver swords.

FAVOR: There was blood everywhere.

NICOLA: And the sound of flesh being cut and torn.

PEASANT 1 (CHARLIE): Help me! I'm dying!

PEASANT 2 (MISKI): I've been stabbed!

TAI: It's mass murder!

MISKI: Run, Charlie! Run!

FAVOR: We're gonna have to swim across that river!

NICOLA: No, there's a boat here. Let's row across it. [aside] We all jumped into the boat, and I grabbed the oars, and rowed for my life.

TAI: Look back there, the peasants are really trying to fight all the king's men.

PADRAIG: But why? Why don't they run like us?

CHARLIE: Maybe they would rather die than pay the king's taxes?

NICOLA: We're across the river. Let's run again!

TAI: I think we can walk now. No one is following us.

FAVOR: Hey look, there's another river in the distance!

NICOLA: Where are we? What just happened?

MISKI: Charlie, stupid idiot he is, set the TimeBook app to land us at the Battle of Deptford Bridge in 1497.

CHARLIE: I thought I would test out the app and see if it worked.

TAI: Yeah, it worked all right and nearly got all of us killed.

PADRAIG: How did you lose your phone, Charlie? Did you get mugged?

MISKI: It wasn't really his fault. A huge bird came along and snatched it out of his hand. We're in 1497, things are a bit different.

FAVOR: Not a black bird, was it?

NICOLA: So, this place right here is Deptford in 1497?

TAI: It must be, but it's weird, it's all fields, and I guess there's a river where the High Street once was.

CHARLIE: Where the High Street is going to be!

FAVOR: I read somewhere that Deptford is called that because it was originally called Deep Water, "Dept" meaning "deep" and "ford" meaning water. So, that river we crossed was the "Deep Water".

PADRAIG: And we were definitely in deep water! We nearly died!

CHARLIE: Hey guys, I need you to give me one of your phones because the first thing I've got to do is find my phone. Thanks, FAVOR. Yes, thank goodness for that, I left my tracking device on. I can see where my phone is. Quick, we all need to hold hands.

FAVOR: I'm not holding his hand! Urr!

MISKI: And I am not holding Favor's hand, they're really dry!

TAI: And I'm certainly not holding Miski's hand! It's all dirty!

NICOLA: And I'm not too keen on holding Tai's hand either.

PADRAIG: And I wouldn't hold any of your hands, even if you paid me! I am going back to school!

CHARLIE: Oh, you guys are pathetic! You won't even help me find my phone!

FAVOR: No, we won't because we need to protect ourselves! Look there's that massive black bird again!

MISKI: And it's diving for us!

TAI: Quick, run!

PADRAIG: [aside] But it was no good.

NICOLA: [aside] The bird had caught us in its massive beak.

CHARLIE: [aside] It had grown.

TAI: Argh! Let me go you horrible bird!

NICOLA: [aside] But it was too late, the bird had caught all of us and there was nothing we could do!

Learning script

TEACHER: OK, we're going to do some Reciprocal Reading based on the passage we have just read. Now, Reciprocal Reading can be done in quite a few different ways; it's main purpose is to get us reading together in a happy, creative way. That's the goal. To get us started though, I am going to ask us to do some writing before we discuss things. We are going to divide up the work so that we as a group can do it much more quickly.

SUMMARIZER: Me and the Teacher are going to work together and answer Question 1, making notes on:

What is this scene about? What is happening in it? How well are we reading, what do we "get" and what don't we "get" and why are we not "getting it"? **(Summarizing)**

QUESTIONER: Me and the Motivator are going to answer these questions:

- Are there any difficult bits we don't understand? Is anything not very clear? If so, can other people in the group help us understand the scene better? **(Clarifying)**

- Does anyone have any questions to ask about the passage **(Questioning)**

ASSESSOR: Me and the Learning to Learn Chief (L2LC) are going to answer these questions:

- What does everyone think might happen next? Is there anything that is NOT said in the scene/passage that we think might be important to consider? **(Predicting/hypothesizing)**

TEACHER: And then we are all going to answer this question:

- How well are we reading? What could we do to improve our reading? **(Evaluating/learning to learn)**

ASSESSOR: Once we have written our answers to our allocated questions in our Learning Journals, we are going to discuss our answers.

QUESTIONER: But why are we writing this stuff down first of all, why can't we just discuss it all?

TEACHER: You have a chance to discuss your answers in your pairs, and then we will have a group discussion. I think it is important for us to get into the practice of writing.

SUMMARIZER: When you write stuff down you think differently from when you discuss things: you can have thoughts that you wouldn't have if you had just discussed things. Writing things down helps consolidate things in your mind. Can I suggest that you have a go at mind-mapping or visual organising your ideas if you like?

A summary might look a bit like this:

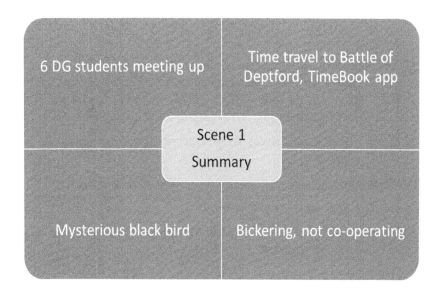

Or you could do it as a flow chart, charting the order in which things happen…

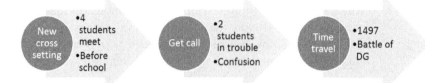

MOTIVATOR: And you have the feeling of having achieved something! And I like the fact that we don't have to answer all the questions by writing them down, we have divided the work up. It's like we are one huge big brain all together!

ASSESSOR: And I can assess from your writing how hard you are working.

TEACHER: OK, can we report back when we've done that writing?

Everyone should do their writing tasks.

TEACHER: OK, once we've done that, we going to hear people's views on every question.

QUESTIONER: Isn't this a very slow way of doing things? Asking everyone!

MOTIVATOR: We are going slowly to begin with, but as you get the hang of Reciprocal Reading, we will speed up.

ASSESSOR: In fact, the point of Reciprocal Reading is that you learn to do all the stages in your own head very quickly when you read difficult passages.

SUMMARIZER: I didn't find the reading difficult at all.

MOTIVATOR: Speak for yourself, I did, I thought it was quite confusing! I found it difficult to imagine what was going on!

TEACHER: That's why we are working as a group; we all have different abilities and attitudes towards reading. We need to encourage each other.

MOTIVATOR: And motivate each other, not say how stupid we are!

ASSESSOR: Yes, I am going to make notes and assess people who are working well – and those who are not, I will give a tick when someone makes a good point, and when someone is unhelpful, I will write a cross.

QUESTIONER: And give us all a detention? You're not a Teacher, you can't do that!

TEACHER: That's true, the Assessor can't give detentions, but they can assess people, and they then have a duty to report back to us about how we are doing.

MOTIVATOR: And together we can work out how to improve. It's not about detentions and punishment, it's about getting us to become better readers. We all want that, don't we?

SUMMARIZER: Yes, I guess we do. But I think we should all make sure that the Assessor is fair in their assessment of us.

MOTIVATOR: And motivating!

TEACHER: One of the biggest problems people have with their reading is not that they are bad at it, but because they don't like it.

SUMMARIZER: Yes, you talked about that before.

TEACHER: And we all need to work together to help each other enjoy reading more.

QUESTIONER: Can't we get on with the work now?

TEACHER: OK, let's do that. Using your notes can we all discuss the key questions. So everyone of us is going to say what we think in answer to these questions:

What is this scene about? What is happening in it? How would you sum up your understanding of thee passage? Did you get most of it? If so, why and how? Were the bits you didn't get, if so why did this happen? Do you need to re-read any bits? Do you need help from other people?
(Summarising your understanding)
Are there any difficult bits we don't understand? Is anything not very clear? If so, can other people in the group help us understand the scene better? **(Clarifying)**

*Does anyone have any questions to ask about the passage **(Questioning)**
What does everyone think might happen next? Is there anything that is NOT said in the scene/passage that we think might be important to consider?
(Predicting/hypothesizing)
How well are we reading? What could we do to improve our reading? **(Evaluating/learning to learn)***

ASSESSOR: Can the Assessors report back to the group as to how people got on?

MOTIVATOR: And can the Motivators, motivate the group by giving them motivating comments and doing motivating things such as saying "Well done!" when someone gives a good answer, or "good try", "nice effort", and clapping if someone does particularly well, or giving a reward such as a smiley face on their learning journal, a nice comment in their learning journal, sticker or little sweetie (if you're allowed in class!).

QUESTIONER: Can the Questioners make sure that everyone is being questioned carefully and that they are being asked open questions such as "What is this passage about?" "What do you mean?" "Can you tell more about that?" "What do you think?" "What do you think the consequences for that is?" "Where's the evidence for that?" "Can you explain how the evidence proves your point?"

ASSESSOR: And can the Assessors be giving feedback to people as to how they are doing such as saying "You seem to have understood the scene really well" or "You don't seem to be saying much about this point" or "Are there any areas you are stuck on which we can help you with?" The Assessor is there to assess how well you're doing and then work out how to improve.

SUMMARIZER: Can the Summarizer make summaries of the key points people have made, noting them down in their Learning Journal if necessary.

LEARNING TO LEARN CHIEF: Can the L2LC note down important terminology and words people are using or should use. Common terms in English are: analysis, explanation, imagery, metaphors, similes, personification, onomatopoeia, rhetorical questions, dialogue, dramatic scenes, dramatic irony, irony etc. Has anyone managed to use any key terminology when discussing things.

Learning Activities

Set some reading Learning intentions, reading more challenging material.
- How? By reading material that interests and motivates you.
- How? By talking to people who know what that more challenging material might be: TEACHERs, other pupils, librarian, parents, carers.
- When? Set some deadlines for talking to people, researching, reading.
- What? Choose some reading material you want to read.
- Why? Think about WHY you are reading this material.

E.g. Over the weekend I will review the books I am reading, and think about what might challenge me further.

Assessment point

To what extent were you Learning intentions met?

Learning intentions: to learn about what Reciprocal Reading is and how it helps you learn; to learn about the different group roles and why they will help you learn

Grade yourself:

Learning intention	Unsatis-factory	Requires improve-ment	Good	Outstand-ing	Targets
To learn about what Reciprocal Reading is					
How RR helps you improve your reading					
To learn about the different group roles and why they will help you learn					

Independent study

In your Learning Journals and Files, collect notes, print outs, articles etc on the following. Choose ONE or more of the following to do:
- Find out more about time travel stories. Why do people like them? What do you think of them?
- Find out more about your local area, and think of time travel stories you could set in your own area.
- Find out more about time generally, find out about when time was discovered as a concept.

Further research

Go to the library and find a book that interests you that links to the theme of time. This could be a book set in the past. If you like sports for example, you could find out about the history of a football team you like, or the history of football generally. Or you could read a time-travel story. Bring this as a wide reading book to these lessons and read it silently when you have nothing else to do, e.g. at the beginning of lessons. As you read it, note down in your learning journal your thoughts and feelings about what you are reading, keeping a reading journal about what is happening and what you like about the book.

A particular topic you could look at is the history of New Cross:

New Cross during World War II:

http://bombsight.org/explore/greater-london/lewisham/new-cross/
http://www.bbc.co.uk/history/ww2peopleswar/stories/86/a2920286.shtml
http://www.eastlondonlines.co.uk/2014/12/new-cross-remembrance-of-world-war-ii-bombing/

The New Cross fire of 1981:

https://en.wikipedia.org/wiki/New_Cross_house_fire

Evaluating

Write about how you are finding the Reciprocal Reading so far, outlining your thoughts and feelings about how it went in the lesson. Discuss your thoughts and feelings with your friends, carers/parents and TEACHER.

Watch some time-travel films, TV programmes and review them.

If your carers etc. up a blog for your group, and note down your thoughts/feelings about Reciprocal Reading.

Lesson 2

Mindful reading meditation

Before starting your reading for the lesson, make sure you do a short mindfulness meditation to help develop your ability to set some clear reading intentions, to pay attention and adopt a positive attitude. Please see the section **Becoming a Mindful Reader** if you have forgotten how to do this.

Learning intentions

Learning intentions	Learning Charm	How?	What?
I intend to learn more about Reciprocal Teaching/Reading		By reading the lesson carefully, by following the instructions, by asking if I don't understand; by having a go at it and reviewing what I have learnt	Discussion work; written notes.
I intend to learn more about summarizing, questioning, clarifying and predicting.		By reading the script and asking about these things, discussing them.	By taking notes of these things.
I intend to learn more about what we mean by reading the world and words.		By thinking deeply about what we mean by reading, asking questions.	Discussion; taking notes; answering the exercises.

Please read through your targets from last lesson and see if there is anything else you need to learn more about. Have a brief discussion about what you feel you need to improve with your reading and how you might improve your reading this lesson, e.g. by re-reading, by looking up difficult words, by having more of a positive attitude, to read with more expression, to think more deeply about what you are reading, to challenge yourself by reading more challenging material in your own time and bring that reading to the lesson to read when you finish the work or at the start of the lessons etc.

Are there any other things you intend to learn about? Please discuss and/or note them down...

Learning script

TEACHER: OK, guys, we've had a go at Reciprocal Reading for the first scene. Let's quickly discuss what we learnt from doing that.

QUESTIONER: Why are we learning about Reciprocal Reading?

MOTIVATOR: I think it's motivating to work together on our reading. I like reading in a group; it's much nicer than reading by yourself.

ASSESSOR: But it will also help us read by ourselves if we get plenty of practice at reading.

SUMMARIZER: I would say we learnt a lot last lesson because we learnt about the process of Reciprocal Reading, and about the script too.

LEARNING TO LEARN CHIEF: We learnt some important vocabulary such as Reciprocal and Reciprocity. Quick test: what do they mean?

TEACHER: Everyone should have a go at answering this question.

QUESTIONER: What's next?

TEACHER: Well, now we've got the hang of Reciprocal Reading, hopefully we can do this for every scene we read and we won't have to explain it again and again.

ASSESSOR: We're going to continue reading the script and start to look closely at it.

MOTIVATOR: And learn about how to enjoy the process of reading.

SUMMARIZER: And learn about what reading is because reading is a lot more than just reading marks on the page, it's about interpreting things, finding meaning in them.

TEACHER: And this script is deliberately designed so that people think about the world around them and learn to "read the world" as well as "reading the page".

QUESTIONER: What does that mean, "reading the world"?

LEARNING TO LEARN CHIEF: That's the first thing we do when we grow up as babies and young children, isn't it? We start to read the world around us. We read people's faces: we see that when they smile they are happy, and when they frown, they are sad.

ASSESSOR: We read the weather: we feel the cold and look at the sky, we feel the sunshine and enjoy the warmth.

TEACHER: In a certain sense, we read everything around us!

LEARNING TO LEARN CHIEF: But we are just reading marks on the page.

ASSESSOR: And bringing all our thoughts, feelings, interpretations to those marks and making those marks on the page create pictures in our minds, making us feel and think things as we read those marks.

MOTIVATOR: Reading is quite magical when you think of it like that. We take these weird signs and create whole worlds out of them: characters, settings, people, ideas, feelings.

TEACHER: Exactly, so let's go on with reading the story!

Scene 2: Meeting the Time Devil

TAI: [aside] And suddenly we materialised in a cobble stone court right next to an old building with a tower.

PADRAIG: Where are we?

FAVOR: We are standing on the Greenwich Meridian line.

NICOLA: It divides the East part of the globe from the West I think.

CHARLIE: And is at the centre of our time zones.

MISKI: But there's no one here. Normally it's heaving with tourists!

PADRAIG: Why is there all this mist and fog? I can't even see down the hill.

TAI: Look out CHARLIE! There is a huge bird diving at you!

PADRAIG: What's happened to Charlie?

FAVOR: He's turned into a huge black bird!

NICOLA: Is that some sort of giant raven?

MISKI: That was so disgusting. The huge bird just sort of entered Charlie! Charlie, are you there?

CHARLIE: CHARLIE has temporarily vacated the premises of his body, and he is now occupied by me, the Greenwich Time Devil!

PADRAIG: What is the Greenwich TIME DEVIL when he or she's at home?

CHARLIE/TIME DEVIL: I mess around with time in the area.

NICOLA: Mess around with time? Like do nasty stuff to time?

CHARLIE/TIME DEVIL: Charlie signed up to TimeBook and friended me. I have lived for about 4 billion years, and no one ever done it. Then Charlie came along last night, and I can finally have some fun!

FAVOR: Err, what kind of fun?

TIME DEVIL: You already had some, didn't you? I mean, you got to see peasants get slaughtered by their king, just because they didn't want him to take all their money and food. I am so sad that I really think it's time to laugh out loud!

TAI: We say "LOL" in the 21st century, Time Devil.

TIME DEVIL: Hey, you can't criticize me for being out of fashion, because I have been asleep for a few billion years.

FAVOR: Seeing innocent people getting murdered by a tyrant is not my idea of fun, Time Devil!

TIME DEVIL: Charlie did request to be at the Battle of Deptford Bridge.

PADRAIG: He did that through TimeBook, didn't he? What do you have to do with TimeBook? What exactly are you up to, Time Devil?

TIME DEVIL: Oh, you are getting so boring with your questions! I think it's time that all six of you had some real fun. You haven't seen anything yet!

FAVOR: [aside] And then there was a rush and a swirling noise, and all six of us could feel ourselves being scattered through time, but not through space; we all, in our different ways, stayed in the same place.

NICOLA: [aside] Just at very different times.

TAI: [aside] It was the scariest thing that ever happened to me.

MISKI: [aside] And the most amazing.

FAVOR: [aside] And the most confusing.

PADRAIG: [aside] And it provoked more questions than answers.

CHARLIE: [aside] And we all got sent to different time periods!

Learning Activities

Carry out Reciprocal Reading based on the scene you have read: explaining what has happened to each other, summing up how well you understood the passage, clarifying any problems you had with it, predicting what might happen next, or filling in the gaps in terms of feeling that there are things that are left out here; asking questions to help each other with summarizing, clarifying, predicting.

Reading the world: brainstorm what time means to you in your world. Write about: What times of the day are your favourite? What times of the year are your favourite? Note down your favourite & least favourite times of the day, week, month, year etc. Who in your life is obsessed by time, e.g. getting places on time, their age etc.? How often do you look at the time and why? When did you learn to read the time? What does time mean to you?

Imagine an article for a parents' magazine called 'Time and the teenager' in which you explain what time means to teenagers today: what their favourite times are, what their least favourite times are, and how parents can help teenagers appreciate the time they have on earth more.

In your Learning Journal, devise a Spider Diagram or vis based on your Reciprocal Reading (RR), summing up what you have discussed in your RR: e.g. what has happened in the scene and what you understand and don't understand in the script, what you want to know more about, what you think might happen next, what you are learning about your learning, and any other points discussed.

In your Learning Journal, write a prediction of what is going to happen next.

In your Learning Journal, note down what strategies are helping you improve your reading and why: re-reading passages you have skipped over or not concentrated upon, or found difficult; getting help and encouragement from other people in the group; thinking about things that interest you and relating them to the script; researching an aspect of the script in more detail.

Assessment point

To what extent were you Learning intentions met:
Learning intentions:
Grade yourself:

Learning intention	Unsatis-factory	Requires improvement	Good	Outstanding	Targets
To learn more about Reciprocal Teaching; to learn more about: summarizing questioning, clarifying, predicting.					
To learn about what we mean by reading; reading the world and words.					
Any goals you set for yourself:					

Independent study

- Continue reading another book/text related to the theme of time travel, noting down in your Learning Journal: what is happening in the book, what you like about it, what you think might happen next.
- Keep a list of useful vocabulary to learn and love.
- Find out about the National Maritime Museum by going on its website and skimming/scanning what is in the collection, why people might want to visit there, what interests you about the museum.
- Write about how you are finding the Reciprocal Reading so far, outlining your thoughts and feelings about how it went in the lesson. Discuss your thoughts and feelings with your friends, carers/parents and teacher.
- Watch some time-travel films, TV programmes and review them.
- If your carers etc. up a blog for your group, and note down your thoughts/feelings about Reciprocal Reading.

Lesson 3

Mindful reading meditation

Before starting your reading for the lesson, make sure you do a short mindfulness meditation to help develop your ability to set some clear reading intentions, to pay attention and adopt a positive attitude. Please see the section **Becoming a Mindful Reader** if you have forgotten how to do this.

Learning intentions: skimming and scanning

Learning intentions	Learning Charm	How?	What?
I intend to learn more about how to skim and scan texts so that I can guess in an informed way about what a text might be about, and how its structure and form shape its meaning and content. (Skimming)		By reading the lesson carefully, by following the instructions, by discussing with people in my group.	Discussion; notes; answering the set tasks.
I intend to learn more about how to guess in an informed way about what a text might be about, and how its structure and form shape its meaning and content. (Skimming)		Through doing the different activities set, and reviewing what I have learnt.	Discussion; note-taking; answering the set tasks.
I intend to learn more about finding information quickly by scanning through texts to look for what I need		Through doing the different activities set, and reviewing what I have learnt.	Discussion; note-taking; answering set tasks.

to know.			
I intend to learn about how to skim and scan in a critical way: questioning whether I am getting the information I need and questioning whether the information I am getting is useful.		Through doing the different activities set, and reviewing what I have learnt.	Discussion; note-taking; answering set tasks.

Please read through your learning intentions from last lesson and see if there is anything else you need to learn more about. Have a discussion about what you feel you need to improve with your reading and how you might improve your reading this lesson, e.g. by re-reading, by looking up difficult words, by having more of a positive attitude, to read with more expression, to think more deeply about what you are reading, to challenge yourself by reading more challenging material in your own time and bring that reading to the lesson to read when you finish the work or at the starts of lessons etc.

Are there any other things you intend to learn about? Please discuss and/or note them down...

Definitions

Skim-reading is when you flick over a text quickly, trying to work out what it is about quickly.

Scanning is when you read a text with a particular purpose in mind, i.e. you want to find a particular piece of information.

When and why?

When might you want to skim and scan texts?
Why is it such a useful skill?
Which texts would you want to skim and scan, and when/why:
- The webpages of a news website for the latest news
- A revision guide.
- A series of instructions about how to use some machinery/technology.

- Recipes for dishes you want to cook.
- A long novel.
- A play.
- A collection of poems in a poetry book.
- Social media site about your friends' activities/views.
- Twitter stream.

Have a Reciprocal Teaching discussion in your group about these points before you read on, with the Teacher making sure that everyone has clear learning intentions for this lesson, and that everyone knows what we mean by skimming and scanning.

Key points: skimming and scanning are vital skills in the modern world. We are bombarded with information all the time: we need to be able to process information quickly, summing it up in a reasonable way in our minds without having to read it in depth.

Key points

Use titles of poems, chapters, books to guide you as to what they are about.

Use chapter headings as the main topics for your notes.

Use the index of a book to find quickly what information you want.

Use CNTRL + F on the computer to find key words.

Strategies

Using your fingers, eyes and body

All of the following strategies about encouraging you to read with your whole body. With books, it is very useful to use your fingers and hands to flick through pages, and run your fingers along lines of text; this helps you focus. There are hundreds of millions of neurons (cells that connect to the brain) in the hand which may mean that using your hands during your reading may help you process the information better. Whatever the scientific evidence, there is no doubt that using your fingers during reading helps you keep focus; this is common sense. So these exercises are simple ones that can be easily done which are also fun. Have a go at them, and see if they work for you. If they don't, do not worry, try and find your own methods for skimming and scanning. If they do, try and adapt them so that you use them when you next skim and scan texts.

Warm-ups: reading the world with your senses

- Skim your eyes all around the room you are in and try to remember as many objects as possible. Now, without looking, write down a list of all you saw in a minute or so.
- Get some small objects (at least 8-10) in your group and shut your eyes and say to the group what you can remember.
- With your eyes shut, get someone to mix up the objects or add new ones, skim your hands over the objects, touching them, then say what they are.
- With your eyes shut, scan the objects to find the one which is your favourite objects. Then least favourite. Then put the objects in rank order of what you like/dislike. Open your eyes.
- Do the above task with your eyes open if it is too difficult with your eyes shut.
- Shut your eyes, and skim the room with your ears, and note down as many sounds as you can hear in 30 seconds.
- Shut your eyes, and scan thee room with your ears, finding your favourite and least favourite sound.
- Shut your eyes, and with a partner who has their eyes open, get them to give your 4-5 very small, quick tastes of food: skim the food. Guess what they are.
- Do the same as above and judge what is your favourite and least favourite food.
- Shut your eyes if you like, and skim the room you are in for all the different smells in it. Write them down or tell them to your group.
- Shut your eyes if you like, scan the room for your favourite or least favourite smells.

Review

What did you learn from doing this exercise? What did you learn about skimming and scanning with the senses? Does it make a difference which order you do things? Do you think it is best to skim first then scan? What did you learn about reading from doing these exercises?

Text based exercises for skimming and scanning

Skim word football

Passing: with your finger randomly pick a word on a page and "pass" to your partner, who picks a word related to the other word in some way, and says the word, nothing more. The pass happens because both players have said the words and agree silently that the words are related. They do not have to say why the words are related. Players should "pass" words in a book for a bit before trying to score a goal so that they get to know the text quickly.

The goal happens when a person the connection between the words, e.g. Word 1: scream, Word 2: horror P2 says both words suggest something frightening is going on in the text. You score a goal for each point you make.

You win a match by scoring 5 goals and then summarizing what you think the text is about using some of the words that have been skimmed.

Scan word football

The same as "skim" football except the Teacher says what words score the goal, e.g. horror words, funny words.

Skimming and scanning shoot 'em up

- Take aim at a word and shoot it dead by showing that you know what it means.
- 1 point for a simple word or phrase
- 2 point for a more complicated word or phrase
- 3 points for a very complicated word or phrase

Skimming and scanning tennis

The same as skimming and scanning football except that you serve by flipping over to a new page; a rally is won by scoring a goal (see previous slide) and the scoring is tennis scoring, e.g. 15 Love etc.

Why? The structure of the tennis game makes the game "finite".

Parachuting into enemy territory

Your mission is to parachute straight into the middle of enemy territory and get to know the "lie of the land" there by becoming like a local: reading the text for a while so that it is like you have read the whole book. Take a difficult book get your plane to sail over the pages as you flick through them and then choose your landing spot, and then parachute in, staying a while in enemy territory by reading it carefully and acting as though you know what is going on and you can speak the language.

SAS operation: take the most important words hostage

A variation on parachuting, except that when you parachute in, you aim to take the most important phrases hostages as quickly as possible, storming pages like the SAS might break into an enemy stronghold, with your copter waiting to lift out the words very quickly for interrogation after you have gone into the page.

Bomb disposal for skimming and scanning

You are a bomb disposal expert who has to diffuse the "bombs" of difficult words. Look carefully through your text like a bomb disposal expert scanning the ground and then when you find a difficult phrase have a go at "diffusing" it by working out quickly what you think it might mean based on the words around it. If you work out the meaning of the phrase, you have diffused the bomb and get a medal!

Treasure Hunt for scanning

Use your finger and make the sound of a metal detector as you move quickly along the text you want to scan: when you believe you have found the information you want (your treasure) make a bleeping sound.

Sky diving

Like a skydiver float with your finger above the pages of a book, looking quickly at each page from a distance without diving into it. Sky dive a whole book in a few minutes. Sky dive lots of books within minutes.

Armed robbery of titles and chapter headings

Arming yourself with the overall purpose of a book beforehand, raid all the titles/chapter headings and work out what it is about using only them. E.g. with a Poetry Anthology, look at the authors/titles of poems, any relevant dates, topics, and work out what the whole anthology is about within minutes, judging what might be the best poems to study in depth.

Plucking low hanging fruit: first and last words

Pluck the low-hanging fruit of the first words and sentences of paragraphs, reading only them, and reading the chapter of a book by only doing this; see if you can work out the meaning of the chapter/section using these low-hanging fruits.

- Do the same for last words of paragraphs.
- Do both: pluck the low-hanging fruit of first and last words of the section you are reading.

Texts for skimming and scanning

Could you choose the texts for skimming and scanning; these could be ones in other subjects, or ones which your TEACHER feels you need practise with skimming and scanning.

You could skim and scan this text if you like.

- Skim this text and work out its overall structure, what it is about, its audience and its purpose. 5-10 minutes.
- Scan this text and find out what the key learning intentions are in the text, making a mindmap of them in your books. 5-10 minutes.

Review

How helpful did you find these strategies? What did you learn from taking these approaches?

Learning script

TEACHER: What strategies help you read?

QUESTIONER: Why is it important to learn about reading strategies? Why can't we just get on and read?

ASSESSOR: As was said in the sections on mindful learning and mindful reading, I would say it is more than strategies that help you read, it's actually your attitude that is important as well. If you are feeling confident and interested in your reading, then you're much more likely to read well.

MOTIVATOR: Yes, we have to be motivated to read. What things are people here motivated to read?

Free discussion where people discuss what they enjoy reading.

SUMMARIZER: So, could everyone write in their Learning Journals what things motivate them to read.

LEARNING TO LEARN CHIEF: And we can we also thinking about different types of reading. There's skimming, scanning, reading quickly, reading slowly, reading with a set of questions in mind, reading to analyze a passage, reading for yourself, reading with other people. It wasn't until quite recently that people actually were required to read by themselves.

MOTIVATOR: When stories were first published hundreds of years ago, people used to read to each other and there was very little reading by yourself partly because books were expensive and people couldn't afford their own copies but also because reading together is really fun, and people enjoyed reading aloud together.

TEACHER: Well anyway, can you discuss:

1. When/why you read quickly, skimming over information. Think about how you read websites/social media here. How do you feel about this type of reading?
2. When/why you read slowly and re-reading. Think about topics you are really interested in. Why might you read slowly, or re-read passages. How do you feel about this type of reading?
3. When/why you might read just to get the meaning of a passage. How do you feel about this type of reading?
4. When/why you might read to analyse a passage. How do you feel about this type of reading?

Scene 3 Charlie: Prince Frederick's Barge, April 1736

CHARLIE: [aside] After the Time Devil whirled me around in space and time, I was sucked into a great wind, and then suddenly I found myself sitting on a long golden boat in the middle of a museum. A museum attendant was running towards me.

MUSEUM WORKER 1 (FAVOR): Hey, sonny, you are not allowed to climb on the exhibits. That is proper gold leaf, you'll ruin it if you clamber all over Prince Frederick's barge.

CHARLIE: [aside] I looked down and found my phone back in my hand. The TimeBook app was glowing, with the message 'Press me' flashing red. Another museum attendant was running towards me.

MUSEUM WORKER 2 (TAI): Hey, young man, you must get off there right now!

CHARLIE: [aside] I pressed the TimeBook app and saw the surroundings of the museum shiver and dissolve. The boat was bobbing up and down on a big river, the Thames, and I was sitting on some cushions with some other people: very strange looking people dressed in wigs and with powdered faces. The sun was shining and several other boats were sailing beside us with people playing music in them.

PRINCE FREDERICK (PADRAIG): Who on earth are you?

CHARLIE: Who are you?

PRINCE FREDERICK (PADRAIG): Father, can you have this creature thrown overboard immediately! He's appeared here from nowhere and has the presumption to ask me who I am!

KING GEORGE II (NICOLA): Don't you know who Prince Frederick is, my son?

CHARLIE: No, I don't!

KING GEORGE II (NICOLA): Oh, isn't that funny! I have always said he's a bit of a nobody!

PRINCE FREDERICK (PADRAIG): Father, why are you always trying to humiliate me? I am somebody you know, I am your son, and the Prince of Wales.

KING GEORGE II (NICOLA): You're nobody until you're king, my son, and I fear the way you're going, you won't last longer than me. You need to go easy on that wine.

CHARLIE: But I don't know who you are either!

PRINCE FREDERICK (PADRAIG) laughs now: That's even funnier, Father! I'll drink that!

CHARLIE: [aside] I watched as Frederick glugged down a lot of wine straight from the bottle.

KING GEORGE II (NICOLA): You don't know who the king is, my son? Have you gone mad?

CHARLIE: I'm sorry but I was put here by…[aside] Just at that moment, the TIME DEVIL emerged from the sky and settled on Frederick's shoulder. Frederick was so drunk that he scarcely noticed.

QUEEN CAROLINE: WIFE OF GEORGE (MISKI): Oh George! There's a huge bird on Frederick's shoulder.

PRINCE FREDERICK (PADRAIG): Don't be ridiculous! Why are you and Father always picking on me? Bird on my shoulder, what nonsense!

CHARLIE: [aside] But there was! And just at that moment, it spoke to me. The other characters froze, becoming statues as time stood still for a moment.

TIME DEVIL (FAVOR): Charlie, are you enjoying this scene?

CHARLIE: I'm not sure I am. First I am being chased by museum attendants, and now I'm here! It doesn't make sense.

TIME DEVIL (FAVOR): You're on Prince Frederick's barge in 1736, watching him having a row with his Mother and Father, Queen Caroline and King George II. They didn't get on.

CHARLIE: But why? Why did you put me here, Time Devil?

TIME DEVIL: Well, you could enjoy the lovely music beside you. There's the great composer Handel himself in one of the boats over there, and they're playing the Water Music. Sublime.

CHARLIE: I'm not a great classical music fan to be honest.

TIME DEVIL: Look down beside you.

CHARLIE: Hey, it's a gun!

TIME DEVIL: Better known as a blunderbuss. On the odd occasion, when the fancy takes him, Prince Frederick enjoys taking pot shots at the birds and sometimes people with his big blunderbuss as he drinks more and more.

CHARLIE: OK, I am not liking the sound of that gun going off.

TIME DEVIL: Oh, do buck up! I have something important to tell you! On this barge, you have a unique chance to change history forever.

CHARLIE: What do you mean?

TIME DEVIL: You're from a Dutch family, aren't you?

CHARLIE: Yes. How did you know that?

TIME DEVIL: That doesn't matter. The main thing is that if you killed this drunken idiot in his ridiculous golden barge with that blunderbuss, you'll change history forever. It's called the Butterfly Effect. This is when a relatively small event (although I have to say killing the Prince of Wales is not exactly a small event!) can lead to really big consequences. Basically, if you killed Frederick now, England would not become the great superpower, and instead the Dutch would rule the world, and you know how much more sensible the Dutch are than the English, don't you?

CHARLIE: I suppose the Dutch are much better footballers, and better at speaking languages.

TIME DEVIL: And they don't go across the globe plundering other people's countries, murdering all their enemies and generally messing things up.

CHARLIE: Actually, I do know a little bit about the Dutch, and I do know that they weren't very nice to people who were their enemies; they committed some terrible atrocities: they killed 10,000 ethnic Chinese in 1740, and as recently as 1947, within living memory, they killed hundreds of innocent people in Indonesia.

TIME DEVIL: You are far too well educated for my liking! That said, you have to admit that the Dutch Empire, on balance, destroyed the lives of far fewer people. Some people estimated that nearly 29 million Indians died in the 19th century because of British rule alone; and that's just in one of their colonies. Some say the British invented concentration camps during the Boer War, and tortured and massacred countless people in their pursuit of power, land, and money. The Dutch pale in comparison.

CHARLIE: When you put it like that, it does make you think. Do you mean I could save millions of people dying if I killed this one person?

TIME DEVIL: Yes, the choice is yours. Spare the life of Prince Frederick and consign the Dutch to the dustbin of history, a mere footnote in the annals of the world, and leave the English to dominate everything for hundreds of years... Peace, love and harmony will take over the earth if you do something about it now!

CHARLIE: [aside] And suddenly time unfroze, and I was sitting next to Prince Frederick with the blunderbuss in my hands. A strange madness gripped me. I could change everything by shooting this drunken idiot whining about his mummy and daddy.

PRINCE FREDERICK (PADRAIG): Mother, Father, this boy is pointing the blunderbuss at me!

KING GEORGE II (NICOLA): I order you to drop that weapon.

QUEEN CAROLINE (MISKI): Don't shoot the poor silly baby!

PRINCE FREDERICK (PADRAIG): Mother, I am not a baby, I am twenty-nine!

CHARLIE: [aside] And then I thought, hey, this isn't really a real situation, it felt more like a computer game to me, and I needed to score points in it. So I packed some gunpowder into the barrel of the blunderbuss, rested its heavy metal on my shoulder, took careful aim as he wobbled drunkenly before me and I shot him, blowing a hole in his powdered, pampered body! And then I looked about the sky for the computer screen to register that I had got extra points for killing the Prince, but I realised to my horror that this was not a computer game. I looked at the Time Devil.

TIME DEVIL: Yes, the TimeBook App does that! It can make things feel like a computer game when they are not!

CHARLIE: You mean I have actually killed a real person? God, how can I live with myself?

TIME DEVIL: Yes, look at his stomach, you've shot his guts out. Lovely!

CHARLIE: Are you a complete psycho?

QUEEN CAROLINE: You've killed my poor silly poopsie Frederick! Soldiers, kill this horrible specimen!

KING GEORGE II: I say, you were a bit harsh on the boy, weren't you? I know he's irritating but killing him is a bit thick, isn't it?

CHARLIE: I saw suddenly some red-coated men stand up in another boat, and aim their muskets at me.

SOLDIER I (NICOLA): You heard our queen. Take aim!

SOLDIER II (FAVOR): Fire!

SOLDIER III (PADRAIG): Kill the traitor!

CHARLIE: [aside] Suddenly there was a huge bang and bullets were whistling past my ears, the smell of gunpowder in my nostrils. I looked in horror at the Time Devil, who grinned a nasty crow-like grin at me.

TIME DEVIL: Don't worry, the deluxe version of the TimeBook app comes bundled with a special all-in-one virus, disease and violent death protection plan; I was good enough to buy you and your friends that so most of attempts at killing you should fail.

SOLDIER II: Take aim and fire again!

SOLDIER I: Aim cross bows at him as well.

CHARLIE: Are you sure it comes with that protection plan?

TIME DEVIL: It is true I couldn't afford the Deluxe Extra plan which is 100% protective. The Deluxe plan is only 85% protective. Some very good attempts at your life could, well, theoretically succeed...

CHARLIE: What? That soldier there looks like he's very keen and rather good at his job!

SOLDIER III: That nearly got him in the eye!

CHARLIE: TIME DEVIL, I want the Deluxe Extra Protection Plan now! They are going to kill me. That nearly hit me! I'm terrified. This is so real. Oh dear, what have I done? [aside] Suddenly everything went black and I was falling through space...

Learning Activities

Carry out Reciprocal Reading based on the scene you have read: explaining what has happened to each other, summing up how well you understood the passage, clarifying any problems you had with it, predicting what might happen next, or filling in the gaps in terms of feeling that there are things that are left out here; asking questions to help each other with summarizing, clarifying, predicting.

Skimming a text

Skim **all** the reading you have done so far. Write down in 2 sentences a summary of the script based on your skimming.

Scanning a text

Now **scan** the text for a particular **purpose** which is to find out what Reciprocal Reading is; you need to scan through the text and find out more about Reciprocal Reading and also reinforce what you have already learnt. Do a Spider Diagram which highlights in your own words and symbols/drawings what Reciprocal Reading is.

Learning to learn moment

What have you learnt about skimming and scanning a text here? How might skimming and scanning help you with your reading in all subjects and outside school? When do you do it naturally?

In your Learning Journal, devise a Spider Diagram of what has happened in the scene.

In your Learning Journal, write a prediction of what is going to happen next.

In your Learning Journal, note down what strategies are helping you improve your reading and why: re-reading passages you have skipped over or not concentrated upon, or found difficult; getting help and encouragement from other people in the group; thinking about things that interest you and relating them to the script; researching an aspect of the script in more detail.

Assessment point

To what extent were you Learning intentions met:
Learning intentions:
Grade yourself:

Learning intention	Unsatis-factory	Requires improve-ment	Good	Outstand-ing	Targets

What else did you learn? What do you think you should improve upon the most, and how might you do this in future lessons?

Independent study

- Find out about the Butterfly Effect: you can find out about here: **https://en.wikipedia.org/wiki/Butterfly_effect** and do some Reciprocal Reading on this Wikipedia entry.

- Have a discussion about computer games and reality: do you think violent computer games make people more violent, and think that they are living in a computer game? Do some Reciprocal Reading of these webpages: **http://www.bbc.co.uk/news/technology-33960075**
- Debate: think critically about the script you have read. Does the script present the British or Dutch fairly? Is it too biased in favour of the Dutch? Is its tone inappropriate: is it too "flippant" (uncaring) and "silly" about some very important issues? Do writers have the right to take true historical incidents like this and turn them into wild stories? What is the point of doing this? Think of films, plays, books that you know of which have taken "true" historical events and made entertaining stories out of them; is this a good thing to do? Why do writers do this?
- Continue reading another book/text related to the theme of time travel, noting down in your Learning Journal: what is happening in the book, what you like about it, what you think might happen next.
- Keep a list of useful vocabulary to learn and love.
- Find out about the National Maritime Museum, and Prince Frederick's barge in particular, by going on its website and skimming/scanning what is in the collection, why people might want to visit there, what interests you about the museum. Have a go a skimming and scanning parts of the website, and reflecting upon how you have improved your skimming and scanning skills.
- The link for Prince Frederick's barge is here: **http://www.rmg.co.uk/see-do/we-recommend/attractions/prince-fredericks-barge**
- Write about how you are finding the Reciprocal Reading so far, outlining your thoughts and feelings about how it went in the lesson. Discuss your thoughts and feelings with your friends, carers/parents and TEACHER.
- Watch some time-travel films, TV programmes and review them.
- If your carers etc. up a blog for your group, and note down your thoughts/feelings about Reciprocal Reading.

Lesson 4

Mindful reading meditation

Before starting your reading for the lesson, make sure you do a short mindfulness meditation to help develop your ability to set some clear reading intentions, to pay attention and adopt a positive attitude. Please see the section **Becoming a Mindful Reader** if you have forgotten how to do this.

Learning intentions: questioning

Learning intentions	Learning Charm	How?	What?
I intend to develop my ability to answer questions		By reading the lesson carefully, by following the instructions, by observing in my group the people who are good at asking questions and learning from them.	By asking questions, by writing down questions
I intend to learn how to ask helpful closed and open questions.		By learning more about closed and open questions and why/when/how you might ask them.	By asking open and closed questions; by writing them down.
I intend to learn how to use questions to motivate myself		By reading the script about this point, and discussing it with members of my group.	To ask questions which motivate me and others to find out more, to learn more.

Please read through your targets from last lesson and see if there is anything else you need to learn more about. Have a discussion about what you feel you need to improve with your reading and how you might improve your reading this lesson, e.g. by re-reading, by looking up difficult words, by having more of a positive attitude, to read with more expression, to think more deeply about what you are reading, to challenge yourself by reading more challenging material in your own time and bring that reading to the lesson to read when you finish the work or at the starts of lessons etc.

Are there any other things you intend to learn about? Please discuss and/or note them down...

Warm-up 1: asking questions about your thoughts and feelings

One really good way of improving your learning is to ask questions about what you are thinking and feeling.

Have a go at doing a **Three-Step Mindfulness Meditation** and remember at the beginning of the meditation (30 seconds-1 minute) to ask yourself in a kind way, "what am I feeling?" "what am I thinking?"

Once you have finished the meditation, do some Free-Mapping or Writing where you ask a series of questions about what you are feeling and thinking by asking OPEN questions (there is no definite answer). Here are some suggestions:

- What am I feeling?
- What was I feeling before this lesson?
- What am I worried about?
- What am I looking forward to?
- What makes me feel good?
- Have a go at asking some closed questions (where there is a definite answer). Here are some suggestions:
- Am I feeling happy? (Yes/no answer)
- Am I feeling sad?
- Am I feeling worried?
- What label is the best label to describe my feelings right now: angry, sad, happy, disgusted, worried?

Once you have asked the questions, have a go at answering them.

Reciprocal Teaching discussion about questions

Then have a discussion using Reciprocal Teaching: a TEACHER is appointed and asks everyone what questions they come up with and their views on those questions.

Which questions did you like the best? Which questions did you not like? Which questions might best help you get into the mood for learning? When might you use open and closed questions when exploring how you are feeling? Why is it useful to question your feelings when considering your learning?

Warm-up 2: Asking questions about your reading

Write down some questions that will help you:
Work out what you know about the story so far;
Guess what might happen.

Do Reciprocal Teaching on this; a new TEACHER is appointed who asks everyone what questions they have come up with. Then do another round of RT and get the TEACHER to ask everyone what their answers might be.

Then read the script together.

Scene 4 Tai: Battle of Trafalgar, 1805

TAI: [aside] The world went spinning and I found myself in a darkened room standing in front of a huge painting of a ship freighted with cannons, sailors, massive masts and rigging, and another boat in front of that, with loads of drowning people trying to clamber onto it.

SAILOR I (FAVOR): Help me! I'm drowning!

SAILOR II (MISKI): I'm bleeding to death! And drowning too!

SAILOR III (CHARLIE): Remember the highest honour is to do one's duty and die for one's country!

SAILOR IV (NICOLA): Forget that for a barrel of laughs, I would rather live!

TAI: [aside] The painting was alive and I found myself stepping into it, I couldn't help myself. I felt as though I had to save the people in the picture. I felt as though I could do it somehow.

MUSEUM ATTENDANT I (PADRAIG): Hey, you are not allowed to climb into the paintings.

TAI: [aside] But it was too late, I was inside the painting, the Battle of Trafalgar 1805; freezing water engulfed me. I was surrounded by flapping arms, bleeding legs, desperate sailors fighting for their lives. The water was exploding all around us. I swam towards the sailor I saw drowning.

SAILOR I (FAVOR): Oh, thank goodness! You've come to save me! I can't swim you know!

TAI: [aside] I pulled the sailor onto the rescue boat and swam over to another one.

SAILOR II (MISKI): Yes, just get me to the boat and I'll be OK.

TAI: [aside] I gripped the bleeding hands of the sailor and by pushing and pulling, and took him over to the boat.

SAILOR II (MISKI): You saved my life!

TAI: And you're not going to die right now!

SAILOR III (CHARLIE): I'm not? But I wanted to die for my country – or at least I thought I did.

TAI: No, come with me...[aside] with that, I put my hands under the sailor's armpits and then swung him onto the boat. It seemed like the time-travelling had given me superhuman strength. Just then a bird appeared in the sky.

TIME DEVIL (PADRAIG): Yes, you'll find that. One of the advantages of TimeBook is that you are defying the laws of space-time which means you gain superhuman powers when you feel strongly about something. You wanted to save the sailors and your mind, now bolstered by the technology of TimeBook, has given you extra healing powers.

TAI: Not sure I really understand what you mean, but I'll go along with it because it's quite nice being so strong!

TIME DEVIL (PADRAIG): Why don't you climb onto my back and we can look at the HMS Victory.

TAI: [aside] And somehow the TIME DEVIL grew bigger and I rose out of the water and climbed onto its back. And together we flew high into the sky, except that it wasn't the sky, it was like we were moving through the ceilings of the museum, which I realised now was the National Maritime Museum. I'd gone there on a school trip and I recognised the exhibits as we flew through the Atlantic Exhibition: Slavery, Trade, Empire and up into the Nelson, Navy Nation Gallery and right slap bang into another huge picture: **The Death of Nelson, 21 October 1805**.

MUSEUM ATTENDANT II (NICOLA): Hey, there are no birds allowed in the museum! I'm warning you, diving into paintings is forbidden!

TIME DEVIL (PADRAIG): I'm afraid you are allowed if you've got the TimeBook app on your phone, mate, didn't you know that?

MUSEUM ATTENDANT II (NICOLA): Are you? Nobody gave me any instructions about a TimeBook app.

TIME DEVIL (PADRAIG): Don't you keep up with new technology? TimeBook is the latest thing, all the kids have got it on their phones. It means you can travel in time and through paintings.

TAI: [aside] And before we could say any more, we were inside a cramped, dark room and I was staring at the great man himself, Lord Admiral Nelson, who was lying half-naked in a sheet, bleeding a great deal as the ship shook and thundered from all the cannon fire from outside.

LORD NELSON (CHARLIE): Who is that Sir Thomas?

SIR THOMAS MASTERMAN HARDY (NICOLA): I am not sure, Admiral.

WILLIAM BEATTY, SURGEON (MISKI): Admiral Nelson, keep still, I need to tend to your wounds.

DR ALEXANDER SCOTT, SHIP'S CHAPLAIN (FAVOR): I fear it may be too late for that, Admiral Nelson. I think it is time that you made peace with your maker, as I am afraid you are about to die.

TIME DEVIL (PADRAIG): So, Tai, look at the scene. The famous death of Nelson. But you, having gathered extra loyalty points from the TimeBook app, have been given a very special TimeBook App First Aid Kit. It's a special offer, just in this time zone. If you go over to him now, and give him a TimeBook App sticking plaster and bandage him up, you will heal him and change English history forever. Nelson will not die.

TAI: You're joking!

TIME DEVIL (PADRAIG): I kid you not! And do you know what the consequences of Nelson living are?

DR ALEXANDER SCOTT (FAVOR): Nelson is a good man, if he lives he will bring much good to the country. He is beloved by all the people, high and low, he could unite us.

SIR THOMAS MASTERMAN (NICOLA): Yes, Tai use your First Aid Kit, and let him live and make this painting change into the healing of Nelson, not his death.

WILLIAM BEATTY, SURGEON (MISKI): And I will be forever known as the greatest surgeon who ever lived!

TAI: Hey, I thought I was the one about to heal Nelson!

TIME DEVIL (PADRAIG): Sad to say the one thing about TimeBookers is that you don't get to be in the history books. But you can take a selfie!

TAI: I get to have a selfie with the bleeding Lord Nelson, and to heal him, but I don't get to be in the history books? That doesn't make sense!

TIME DEVIL: Well, TimeBookers know that you healed him because your selfie goes on your History, but TimeBook is, well, an exclusive time-space social media thing, and it's only TimeBookers who get to see the truth about history.

TAI: And how many TimeBookers are there?

TIME DEVIL: At the moment, only seven.

TAI: God, you've got a lot of catching up to do with Facebook!

TIME DEVIL: Ah but it's not the quantity that counts, but the quality! You're getting to alter human history forever!

TAI: [aside] I'm not sure what will happen if Nelson lives, but hey, I think he seems like a good guy to me, so I'm going to do it. Well, here goes, this First Aid Kit looks like any other First Aid Kit to me, like the ones we have in school. I'm not sure that this sticking plaster and bandage will make any difference. These are bloody wounds: he's been shot through the shoulder and the spine! His back looks like it's all smashed in. It's horrible!

TIME DEVIL (PADRAIG): Just put two plasters on the two major wounds and then wrap his shoulder and lower back in bandages.

WILLIAM BEATTY: Here, let me help you. I'll use this plaster for his lower back and wrap that, and you can do the shoulder.

TAI: OK, but I'm getting all covered in blood! It's all warm and sticky! Yuck!

TIME DEVIL: There are some special wet wipes in the First Aid Kit; they'll help clean you up when you're finished.

Lord Nelson (CHARLIE): What are these bandages that I'm being wrapped in? Oh my goodness, I am suddenly feeling much, much better!

WILLIAM BEATTY, SURGEON (MISKI): My surgery has worked, Lord Nelson!

DR (FAVOR): Praise be the Lord God! He has healed you!

TAI: And everyone watched in amazement as Lord Nelson got up from his death bed and smiled.

LORD NELSON (CHARLIE): Victory is ours, we have won the Battle of Trafalgar, and I am very much alive!

TIME DEVIL (PADRAIG): Ha, ha, ha! You have no idea how much you've messed up the history books TAI! Just think: there's no Nelson's column in Trafalgar Square because of this! There are no pictures of the death of Nelson and he becomes a bit of a forgotten hero, to be honest. The only person who is happy about it is Emma Hamilton!

TAI: Who's she? Suddenly, a very pretty woman in some very expensive-looking but old fashioned clothes appeared before me...

EMMA HAMILTON (NICOLA): I'm Horatio's beloved! That's who I am! We're not married, but we love each other!

DR ALEXANDER SCOTT, CHAPLAIN: Oh dear! That damn Hamilton woman! She'll continue prancing around London society like a queen now! In the other parallel universe, she was humiliated when Nelson died; he was the only thing that kept her from living like a courtesan.

TAI: [aside] Well, that's good. I'm glad that Emma enjoys the rest of her life.

TIME DEVIL: That's the spirit! Mucking up history is really fun, isn't it? But I have to tell everyone here that technically you have ruined Nelson's reputation. Without his death at Trafalgar, he doesn't become nearly as important to the nation as he would dying a hero's death; he goes out with a whimper not a bang!

LORD NELSON: What? But I wanted to die a hero! You mean to say I become a bit of nobody?

TIME DEVIL: Ha, ha, ha! You do!

LORD NELSON: I think this young person needs a lesson, then. Men, can you seize her immediately?

SOLDIER I: I think we need to kill her, she's a traitor; she's tarnished the reputation of the greatest naval hero in history!

LORD NELSON: Yes, we need to get rid of her; I think she's a French spy; an enemy!

SOLDIER I: Men, take aim fire!

TAI: [aside] Bullets whizzed past my ears. Time Devil, they're going to kill me, and I saved Nelson's life!

TIME DEVIL: Don't worry too much, I've bought you the TimeBook Deluxe Protection plan which will protect you against most violent deaths.

DR ALEXANDER SCOTT: Yes, fire at her; we don't want that dreadful woman marching around London society.

SOLDIER I: Fire!

SOLDIER II: Fire again!

SOLDIER I: Smash her to smithereens!

TAI: The bullets do seem to be missing me! Is that the protection plan working, Time Devil?

TIME DEVIL: Yes, it's 85% protective!

SOLDIER I: Shoot her!

TAI: Did you say 85%? That means 15% of the time, I might die?

SOLDIER II: Fire so much that there's nothing left of her head, only bits of brain on the floor!

SOLDIER II: And guts on the floor!

TAI: Someone save me! Help me! One of these bullets is going to hit me!

TIME DEVIL: It's only death, you'll get over it…

TAI: I won't, I don't want to die!

SOLDIER I: Fire, fire, fire! Blast her!

TAI: TIME DEVIL, get me out of here!

TIME DEVIL: I don't think so! I think you need to know what real terror is! Ha, ha, ha!

Learning Activities

Reciprocal Reading

Carry out Reciprocal Reading based on the scene you have read: explaining what has happened to each other, summing up how well you understood the passage, clarifying any problems you had with it, predicting what might happen next, or filling in the gaps in terms of feeling that there are things that are left out here; asking questions to help each other with summarizing, clarifying, predicting.

Write down 5 open questions about the section you have read; write down 5 closed questions. Test each other on these questions.

What questions provoke the most discussion and why? What are the most helpful questions to ask? What questions help you the most and the least?

Have a go at answering these questions.

In your Learning Journal, devise a Spider Diagram of what has happened in the scene.

In your Learning Journal, write a prediction of what is going to happen next.

In your Learning Journal, note down what strategies are helping you improve your reading and why: re-reading passages you have skipped over or not concentrated upon, or found difficult; getting help and encouragement from other people in the group; thinking about things that interest you and relating them to the script; researching an aspect of the script in more detail.

Assessment point

To what extent were you Learning intentions met?
Learning intentions:
Grade yourself:

Learning intention	Unsatis-factory	Requires improve-ment	Good	Outstand-ing	Targets
I intend to develop my ability to answer questions					
I intend to learn how to ask helpful closed and open questions.					
I intend to learn how to use questions to motivate myself					

What else did you learn? What do you think you should improve upon the most, and how might you do this in future lessons?

Independent study

- Do some Reciprocal Reading about the death of Nelson, looking at this real-life account of his death by Dr. William Beatty: **http://www.eyewitnesstohistory.com/lordnelson.htm**
- Find out about the Battle of Trafalgar and Nelson. Why is Nelson such an important person in English history? Where is

there a column devoted to him and a square devoted to Trafalgar? Have you been to this place?
- Write a poem about Nelson and the Battle of Trafalgar, and/or a poem about an important leader who means a lot to you and a conflict, e.g. Nelson Mandela and his battle against apartheid, or Malala and her battle against sexism.
- Continue reading another book/text related to the theme of time travel, noting down in your Learning Journal: what is happening in the book, what you like about it, what you think might happen next.
- Keep a list of useful vocabulary to learn and love.
- Find out about the National Maritime Museum by going on its website and open and closed questions about what you find there.
- Write about how you are finding the Reciprocal Reading so far, outlining your thoughts and feelings about how it went in the lesson. Discuss your thoughts and feelings with your friends, carers/parents and TEACHER.
- Watch some films about Lord Nelson: you find links here to films: **http://www.imdb.com/character/ch0029113/**

G and T Extension
- Try to figure out, by asking open and closed questions, what might have happened if Nelson had lived. For example, you could ask: "Would England have won more battles?" "Would Nelson have influenced British politics?"

Lesson 5

Mindful reading meditation

Before starting your reading for the lesson, make sure you do a short mindfulness meditation to help develop your ability to set some clear reading intentions, to pay attention and adopt a positive attitude. Please see the section **Becoming a Mindful Reader** if you have forgotten how to do this.

Learning intentions: summarizing

To learn more about how to summarize; to learn how to get the overall gist of a passage; to learn how to use a range of strategies to summarize a passage.

Learning intentions	Learning Charm	How?	What?
I intend to learn more about how to summarize passages.		By reading the lesson carefully, by following the instructions, by observing in my group the people who are good at summarizing and learning from them.	By discussing my ideas in my group in a helpful, collaborative way.
I intend to learn more about how to work out the overall gist or meaning of a passage.		By thinking hard about whether I understand the passage for myself.	By writing a summary.
I intend to learn more about the different strategies for summarizing a passage.		By reading the script about this point, and discussing it with members of my group.	By having a go at different ways of doing summaries, e.g. written/spoken, spider-diagrams, bullet points etc.

Are there any other things you intend to learn about? Please discuss and/or note them down...

Activate Prior Knowledge

Please read through your targets from last lesson and see if there is anything else you need to learn more about. Have a discussion about what you feel you need to improve with your reading and how you might improve your reading this lesson, e.g. by re-reading, by looking up difficult words, by having more of a positive attitude, to read with more expression, to think more deeply about what you are reading, to challenge yourself by reading more challenging material in your own time and bring that reading to the lesson to read when you finish the work or at the starts of lessons etc.

Using RT, recap what you have learnt so far and what you think might happen next.

Scene 5 Padraig: The Great Comet 1843

PADRAIG: [aside] And it was crazy, I was spun high up into the air, and then found myself sitting on the back of a huge black bird who swooped down over the fields that changed into a familiar place, Deptford High Street, old houses shimmering and transforming into new ones, and I was flying up the Thames past the Cutty Sark, and straight into a grand white building with an amazing entrance way and an incredible spiral staircase, and I was twisting and turning through doorways, still on the bird's back, terrified I might bash my head on the ceiling because the bird kept ducking down and up, down and up, until we were heading slap bang into a big painting of a tiny man staring up into a great comet lighting up a night sky.

CHARLES PIAZZI SMYTH (NICOLA): Marvellous, isn't it? Absolutely fantastic!

PADRAIG: [aside] I was now right next to a young man, with a strange beard, standing before a painting on an easel in a huge domed room. It was night time.

SIR THOMAS MACLEAR (MISKI): Smyth, what on earth is this young chap doing here? Did you by any chance invite him to see the comet?

CHARLES PIAZZI SMYTH (NICOLA): I didn't Sir Thomas but now that he's here, he might as well have a look!

SIR THOMAS MACLEAR (MISKI): You're not curious as to how he got here? He came from nowhere, Charles.

PADRAIG: [aside] Sir Thomas was a much older man, maybe in his forties, and seemed anxious to get rid of me because I was blocking his view through a big telescope; my face was right against the lens.

SIR THOMAS MACLEAR (MISKI): You boy, why are you standing right in front of my telescope! You're ruining my observation of the comet.

PADRAIG: Sorry…[aside] I stood to one side so that I was not blocking his view through the telescope and saw that that the younger man, Smyth, was so keen on doing his painting that he didn't care what I did. I looked through the gap in the dome which both men were staring through – Sir Thomas with his telescope, Charles with his eyes -- and saw the most incredible light shining in the sky.

CHARLES PIAZZI SMYTH (NICOLA): Isn't that the most beautiful thing you've ever seen in your life?

SIR THOMAS MACLEAR (MISKI): Servants are so ignorant these days! I bet you don't even know what country you're in! In fact, could you go back to the servants' quarters where you came from!

CHARLES PIAZZI SMYTH (NICOLA): Oh, let him stay for a minute or two longer.

PADRAIG: Where am I?

CHARLES PIAZZI SMYTH (NICOLA): You're in the Royal Observatory on the Cape of Good Hope in South Africa my son, and you're witnessing one of the greatest events in the last thousand years!

PADRAIG: [aside] Oh, so I get it! I am inside that painting! In fact, I am inside the painting that Charles is painting right now. That's where the TIME DEVIL sent me! Duh! How stupid am I for not realising that?

SIR THOMAS MACLEAR (MISKI): Boy, you're really not making sense, now get out!

PADRAIG: [aside] Just at that moment, a big bird swooped through from the sky and through the gap in the dome.

CHARLES PIAZZI SMYTH (NICOLA): Go and get a stick or something and get that bird out of my way, he's blocking the view! I won't be able to do my painting! How annoying!

TIME DEVIL (FAVOR): PADRAIG, do you think it's time we gave Charles and Sir Thomas the shock of their lives? Would you like to give them something that they really won't forget?

PADRAIG: I don't trust you TIME DEVIL. What are you planning?

TIME DEVIL (FAVOR): Trust me and you'll see.

PADRAIG: [aside] And then, Charlie, my friend from Deptford Green, tumbled out of the feathers of the TIME DEVIL's wings…Charlie, what are you doing here?

CHARLIE: Don't trust him, PADRAIG, he tricked me into shooting the Prince of Wales!

PADRAIG: [aside] But it was too late! The Royal Observatory began to swivel and dissolve, with the huge South African night sky swallowing up the dome and all its furniture. All of us flew up into the starry space above us: me in my trainers, Charlie with his phone, Smyth with his easel and painting, Sir Thomas with his telescope, and the Time Devil with his black wings.

SIR THOMAS MACLEAR (MISKI): Goodness gracious me Smyth, is it that brandy I drank after dinner which is making me see this, or are we actually flying towards the comet?

CHARLES PIAZZI SMYTH (NICOLA): Hmmnn, I believe we may well be heading towards the comet at a frighteningly fast speed…

CHARLIE: PADRAIG, I feel that this might be even worse than shooting the Prince of Wales. This Time Devil really is a Devil!

PADRAIG: Hey, Time Devil, what are you doing?

TIME DEVIL (FAVOR): I thought you might like to see the comet to end all comets -- which some scientists believe created life on earth!

PADRAIG: [aside] As we neared the light of the comet, we felt ourselves being sucked back in time and now found ourselves sitting on the white-hot tail of a comet, instead of heading towards it. We were going very fast and fire, sparks, ash, smoke and wind whistled past us. It was both hot and cold.

CHARLIE: I can't stop coughing! It's so hot and smoky! It feels like we're on a rollercoaster made of fire and smoke!

PADRAIG: Yes, that's exactly what it feels like that Dracula rollercoaster at Chessington, only much more frightening!

CHARLES PIAZZI SMYTH (NICOLA): What's that fiery volcanic planet down there getting bashed by lots of meteorites?

SIR THOMAS MACLEAR (MISKI): I have no idea. This is a very bad dream. I am not drinking that brandy again!

CHARLIE: Hey, is that the earth just as it was forming billions of years ago?

TIME DEVIL (FAVOR): You're a bright one, aren't you? You're right, it is.

PADRAIG: And don't tell me, this is the comet that specifically brings life to earth? Is that right?

TIME DEVIL (FAVOR): Or not! I'm now giving you, Padraig, the choice; do you give life a miss and spare all of mankind and animal kind and every other kind of creature billions years of misery and toil and struggle, or do you make sure this comet lands on earth and starts the whole primeval soup going?

CHARLIE: You can't give Padraig a choice like that!

TIME DEVIL (FAVOR): I'm a Time Devil and the TimeBook App offers this experience as an add-on extra for those people who have spent the most time on it!

CHARLIE: PADRAIG, have you been spending a lot of time on your phone?

PADRAIG: Well, I...there was nothing else to do when you guys were gone, and I just thought I'd look at the TimeBook App for a bit.

TIME DEVIL: Yes, you didn't notice but, what with space-time being all twisted out of shape, you actually spent nearly 4 billion years on it and didn't look up once!

CHARLIE: Four billion years on your phone! Padraig, that's some addiction you've got!

TIME DEVIL: He was feeling a bit lonely. Anyway, the point is he's now got to make a choice: does he bring life to earth or not? Remember you'll spare countless billions of people and animals terrible suffering if you give life a miss!

PADRAIG: I'm not sure I have enough information to really make that choice!

TIME DEVIL (FAVOR): Oh fine! Be like that! You need to be better educated! How boring! Well, Padraig I'll show you what an education is!

CHARLIE: What do you mean by an education? I thought you got an education in school, not doing crazy stuff like this?

PADRAIG: I think I'm beginning to realize that education is a lot more than school!

TIME DEVIL (FAVOR): Yes, very good point PADRAIG. Now because I want you to really learn some important stuff, I have decided that we're going to return to this moment after we've visited the others in their different time zones. And I think after that you'll be pretty well educated, or educated enough and then PADRAIG will be ready to make the right decision about whether to bestow life on earth.

CHARLES PIAZZI SMYTH (NICOLA): What about Sir Thomas and myself?

SIR THOMAS MACLEAR (MISKI): Can we come too?

TIME DEVIL (FAVOR): Did you befriend me on TimeBook?

SIR THOMAS MACLEAR (MISKI): What are you talking about?

Charles Piazzi Smyth (NICOLA): What's TimeBook?

TIME DEVIL (FAVOR): Sorry chaps, you're not my friends, so I've got to send you back to your old time stream.

PADRAIG: [aside] Charlie and I watched as Charles Piazzi Smyth and Sir Thomas disappeared into the time vortex, kicking and screaming.

CHARLES PIAZZI SMYTH and SIR THOMAS MACLEAR: AARRGHHH!

PADRAIG: But TIME DEVIL, lots of other rocks are hitting this comet; my legs are on fire!

TIME DEVIL: And look at that boulder heading for your chest! When it hits you, your lungs and heart will be red hot rock!

PADRAIG: Arrgh! All of these rocks are hitting me!

ROCK 1: Let's hit, Padraig, isn't it funny to watch him scream?

ROCK 2: Bash, bash, bang!

PADRAIG: Arggh! This is painful!

ROCK 1: Smash, smash, bash, bash we go! Oh what fun!

ROCK 2: Break his legs!

ROCK 1: Crack open his head like an egg!

PADRAIG: TIME DEVIL, save me! Every bone in my body will be broken if you don't do something!

TIME DEVIL (FAVOR): Oh you teenagers are so weak! First Charlie, then Tai, and now you moaning about a bit of violence! Get used to it! This is the essence of history: death and violence. Plus I paid for a special Deluxe Protection Plan for you guys, it protects you against violent death and disease 85% of the time!

PADRAIG: What about the other 15% of the time?

TIME DEVIL: I couldn't afford 100% cover! You people, always wanting the most expensive things!

PADRAIG: This rock has broken my arm I think. I'm in agony!

TIME DEVIL: I think you need to feel the pain of creation, my boy! And this is it!

Learning Activities

Carry out Reciprocal Reading based on the scene you have read: explaining what has happened to each other, summing up how well you understood the passage, clarifying any problems you had with it, predicting what might happen next, or filling in the gaps in terms of feeling that there are things that are left out here; asking questions to help each other with summarizing, clarifying, predicting.

Every member of the group should do ONE of these summarizing tasks.

- Having read the scene, now shut your eyes and replay the scene in your head. What parts leap out at you? Open your eyes and write down the key things that have happened in the passage. How did you find shutting your eyes and taking a "breathing space" to think about the passage?
- Use a highlighter to highlight the important lines in the scene. Using these highlighted bits, write a summary of the scene in your own words. How did you find this approach which is to "edit" down the passage to the important lines/words?
- Ask a specific question of the passage, which could be "What does PADRAIG experience in this scene?" and answer it. How did you find this approach to summarising; i.e. asking a specific question and answering it.
- Visualise the scene, and draw pictures/symbols of the important parts of it; it doesn't matter how good you are at drawing, it's the way you summarise the scene it that is important. How did you find this approach?
- Spider diagram the scene. How did you find this approach?
- Compare and contrast the scene with what has happened before, showing how what happens to PADRAIG is similar and different to what happened to TAI and CHARLIE. How did you find this "compare and contrast" approach to summarising?

In your Learning Journal, devise a Spider Diagram of what has happened in the scene.

In your Learning Journal, write a prediction of what is going to happen next.

In your Learning Journal, note down what strategies are helping you improve your reading and why: re-reading passages you have skipped over or not concentrated upon, or found difficult; getting help and encouragement from other people in the group; thinking about things that interest you and relating them to the script; researching an aspect of the script in more detail.

Assessment point

To what extent were you Learning intentions met:
Learning intentions:
Grade yourself:

Learning intention	Unsatisfactory	Requires improvement	Good	Outstanding	Targets
I intend to learn more about how to summarize passages.					
I intend to learn more about how to work out the overall gist or meaning of a passage.					
I intend to learn more about the different strategies for summarizing a passage.					

What else did you learn? What do you think you should improve upon the most, and how might you do this in future lessons?

Independent study

Look online at the picture The Great Comet 1843. Describe the picture in your own words. What does it make you feel, think and see?

Write your own story or poem about a comet.

Find out about comets and the role they have played in the history of the universe; how they have affected people; watch some documentaries online etc. Summarize your findings and put them in your Learning Journal.

Continue reading another book/text related to the theme of time travel, noting down in your Learning Journal: what is happening in the book, what you like about it, what you think might happen next.

Keep a list of useful vocabulary to learn and love.

Find out about the National Maritime Museum by going on its website and skimming/scanning what is in the collection, why people might want to visit there, what interests you about the museum.

Write about how you are finding the Reciprocal Reading so far, outlining your thoughts and feelings about how it went in the lesson. Discuss your thoughts and feelings with your friends, carers/parents and TEACHER.

Watch some time-travel films, TV programmes and review them.

If your carers etc. up a blog for your group, and note down your thoughts/feelings about Reciprocal Reading.

Lesson 6

Mindful reading meditation

Before starting your reading for the lesson, make sure you do a short mindfulness meditation to help develop your ability to set some clear reading intentions, to pay attention and adopt a positive attitude. Please see the section **Becoming a Mindful Reader** if you have forgotten how to do this.

Activate Prior Knowledge

What do we mean by predicting? What do we mean by hypothesizing? What do we mean by "filling-in-the-gaps"? Why do these skills help you improve your reading?

Learning intentions: predicting, filling in the gaps

Learning intentions	Learning Charm	How?	What?
I intend to learn more about making predictions and why they help you learn better.		By reading the lesson carefully, by following the instructions, by discussing with people in my group.	Discussion; notes; answering the set tasks.
I intend to learn about "filling in the gaps" in our knowledge, and why this is important; spotting the "gaps" and trying to "fill them in"		By thinking hard about what I don't know and how I might find out more.	Discussion; note-taking; answering the set tasks.
I intend to learn more about the different strategies for predicting, hypothesizing and filling in the gaps.		By discussing what strategies help you predict, hypothesize and filling in the gaps.	Discussion; note-taking; answering set tasks.

Please read through your targets from last lesson and see if there is anything else you need to learn more about. Have a discussion about what you feel you need to improve with your reading and how you might improve your reading this lesson, e.g. by re-reading, by looking up difficult words, by having more of a positive attitude, to read with more expression, to think more deeply about what you are reading, to challenge yourself by reading more challenging material in your own time and bring that reading to the lesson to read when you finish the work or at the starts of lessons etc.

Are there any other things you intend to learn about? Please discuss and/or note them down...

Making Predictions

TEACHER: Before reading the scene, can everyone predict again what might happen to NICOLA in the 2nd Opium War; try to make an educated guess based on what has happened before in the script. Think about the title and the clues in the title "The 2nd Opium War: 1856".

Scene 6 Nicola: The 2nd Opium War: 1856

NICOLA: [aside] I was flung through time, I could feel it moving past me, pushing me backwards, through the decades, people race past me in the sky. I watch in astonishment as they got younger and younger, and then disappeared, their clothes changing, their body un-creasing all their wrinkles until they were young children, then babies, then foetuses, then just sperm fertilising the egg, and then nothing…

TIME DEVIL (MISKI): I have given you the best time travelling trip of the lot, haven't I? You're the one who gets to watch people getting younger, and then watch the moment their eggs are fertilised.

NICOLA: TIME DEVIL, you really scare me!

TIME DEVIL (MISKI): That's why I am a Devil and not a God! I love freaking people out! Now watch this!

NICOLA: [aside] I found myself riding on the back of the TIME DEVIL as he flew into what I recognised as the National Maritime Museum, up the stairs, past the huge map of the world on the floor by the café, and into an exhibition space. But then the paintings in the gallery became real, and from being inside the museum, I found myself outside by the river. My nose was attacked by the smell of spices, sugary and savoury; magnificent masts of ships floated by me, sailors climbed the rigging and shouted, "Land ahoy!", and I could see Deptford before me, but it was different, very different, there were lots of old fashioned, wooden ships tied up where Pepy's Park is.

The Time Devil: Teaching & Drama Script

TIME DEVIL (MISKI): Cool, ain't it? That was what Deptford looked like hundreds of years ago. It was where the Royal Navy was first conceived of!

NICOLA: I know this place from walking around near my home and it's all deserted in my own time. I seem to be in the past. Wow! It's so full of activity! I can't believe there are so many ships there!

TIME DEVIL (MISKI): Deptford was where they made the ships for the East India Company.

NICOLA: I know the road up by Lidl, near the Isle of Dogs, the East India Dock road.

TIME DEVIL: The company is long gone now, but once this private company, which had its ships built for it in Deptford, ruled India. Look at the ships unloading their cargo!

NICOLA: [aside] We were standing on Deptford dock watching young boys unloading barrels. One of them had crashed against a big anchor and split open, leaking something sticky.

BOY 1 (FAVOR): Here, you, would you like a lick of this stuff?

NICOLA: [aside] The boy dipped his hand into the sticky stuff and indicated that I should lick his finger.

BOY 1 (FAVOR): What's the matter, do you think I'm dirty or something?

NICOLA: You're filthy! And you stink!

BOY 2 (CHARLIE): Here, don't you cuss my mate! He's the cleanest cabin boy I know!

NICOLA: You're even dirtier!

TIME DEVIL: Dip your finger in the stuff.

NICOLA: [aside] I did, and tasted it! It tasted both bitter and sugary. Ugh, weird.

BOY 1 (FAVOR): Molasses, don't you just love them?

TIME DEVIL (MISKI): And look at the other things they're unloading! Tea, sugar, rum, porcelain, silk and if we look over here in these chests, something very special.

NICOLA: [aside] I opened one of the chests sitting on the wharf and saw it was full of bottles labelled opium, crammed to the top with a sticky brown substance.

BOY 1 (FAVOR): Smoke a bit of that in your pipe, and you'll be as happy as Larry!

BOY 2 (CHARLIE): Yeah, go down to Limehouse and you'll plenty of sailors lying about in a daze! Me, I would never touch the stuff! It ruins your life!

TIME DEVIL (MISKI): He is referring to the fact that during this time some people were addicted to the stuff. In fact, the East India Company had fought two wars just so that they would have the sole right to sell the narcotic to the Chinese.

BOY 1 (FAVOR): Hey, are we going to fight China again?

TIME DEVIL (MISKI): It hasn't happened yet, it's just about to. And I think you, my boy, are going to fight in it!

NICOLA: [aside] There was a whirling noise and together we were catapulted across the globe like we'd been fired out of a cannon. And suddenly, I landed bang on the deck of a ship. I could feel the heat immediately.

BOY 1 (FAVOR): Crikey, watch out mate, the Chinese are lobbing stinkpots at us! Duck and cover your face with your hankie!

NICOLA (coughing): Oh dear, the smell is like a stink bomb or something, and it's making my eyes water.

TIME DEVIL (MISKI): It's Sulphur, it's the kind of chemical warfare the Chinese used in order to stop the East India Company controlling the opium trade.

NICOLA: Where are we? This isn't Deptford! It doesn't look like England at all!

BOY 2 (CHARLIE): We're in the South China Sea mate, and we're fighting on the HMS Nankin! I'm in the Navy now and fighting for Queen and Country for our right to trade freely!

CAPTAIN of the HMS Nankin (TAI): You there, mid-shipmen, get the cannons ready, we're going to fire at the enemy! We're going to demolish them for once and for all! Get ready fire!

NICOLA: [aside] The boys beside me lit the fuses of the cannons which were on the deck of the HMS Nankin and there was a terrific noise and I watched as the cannon balls flew through the hot air, hitting the sides of a stone fort in front of us.

CAPTAIN (TAI): By Jove, I think we got them! Well done boys! A few more rounds and we'll defeat the ruddy enemy!

NICOLA: [aside] But just then, there was a big flash from the walls of the fort opposite us and bang, cannon balls exploded on the deck, hitting the boy right next to me, the one that had shown me molasses in Deptford. His rib cage was smashed in and he lay on the deck, bleeding to death. Suddenly, I saw that PADRAIG was standing beside me, looking very shocked.

PADRAIG: So, this boy has died thousands of miles from home trying to fight a war that enabled the British to deal drugs, is that right, TIME DEVIL?

TIME DEVIL: Something like that. The British Navy supported the East India Company in its war with China.

PADRAIG: But we're taught in school and by our parents that drugs are really bad, so why were the British fighting a war so that they could deal drugs? It's like they are no better than the drug dealers who drive their fast cars around London, terrorizing all the local people.

NICOLA: You could say they were worse. The drug dealers in London are just sad and messed up. The East India Company was backed by everyone, even the Queen and the Navy.

CAPTAIN of the HMS Nankin (TAI): Yes, but we were just trying to make sure that the country stayed wealthy and prosperous. We were doing it for the economy!

PADRAIG: But look at the problems! Lots of people addicted to drugs, lots of wars with many deaths, and misery brought to millions.

NICOLA: Hey PADRAIG, are you, OK? You seem really upset! I mean I'm sad that this boy has died, but it's like I'm in a strange dream.

PADRAIG: This is no dream. This boy really did die because of this war.

TIME DEVIL (MISKI): And Padraig must decide soon whether it is all worth it!

NICOLA: Huh? What's going on?

TIME DEVIL: But Nicola, I do have a little choice for you my dear. First, you need to hop on my back! We're going to fly to India!

NICOLA: Umm…

PADRAIG: Don't do it Nicola, the Time Devil will mess with your head!

TIME DEVIL: Oh, come on, have some fun!

NICOLA: I guess, I need some light relief after the death of that poor boy… [aside] And so I do as I am told and jump on the TIME DEVIL's back, and soon I'm flying over the Indian Ocean, and swooping down over the huge mass of India.

TIME DEVIL: Isn't it beautiful? By the way, if we dive down for a bit, we can see all the opium crops that are being grown here so that the opium can be shipped to the Chinese. Many Indian people used to grow their own produce, feeding themselves, but lots of them grow opium! And there on the Indian Ocean we can see all the ships sailing off to China with the drug packed below decks in barrels.

NICOLA: It's not a great situation, is it?

TIME DEVIL: Well that's 1856 for you! Next year though there is going to be huge revolution in India, many Indians are going to rebel against British control of India and the horrible East India Company. The British called it the Indian Mutiny of 1857, but others call it the First War of Independence.

NICOLA: That's interesting the different words people use. Mutiny makes it sound like something horrible, whereas the War of Independence makes it sound noble.

TIME DEVIL: Exactly! Language is important, but so are weapons. The Indian Mutiny or War of Independence failed and the British killed the people who were the main protestors. We could change that right now. Under my wing, I have the blueprints for a cheap and easy gun for the Indians to make. All we'd need to do would be to drop it into that house down there, where there is a specialist gun maker, and we'd give the rebels a good chance of winning their fight. The choice is yours! Otherwise, the Indians won't achieve independence for nearly another hundred years.

NICOLA: Drop it! Yes, drop it! The Indian people deserve to be free! [aside] But suddenly, I found that a lot English soldiers were gazing at me. I looked down, and there under the Time Devil's wing, were lots of leaflets that had the blueprints that showed people how to make guns. Seized by a strange excitement and a thirst for justice, I grabbed them and flung them towards the ground, watching them flutter towards the Indian villages. However, to my horror, I noticed that it was not Indian people coming out of the homes, but soldiers, who looked suspiciously English.

BRITISH SOLDIER 1: What is this leaflet? It's a blueprint for the Indians to make weapons and calling them to fight for freedom! We can't have this!

BRITISH SOLDIER 2: No, we can't come on men, let's get our cannons and guns and blast this wretched girl and her bird out of the sky!

BRITISH SOLDIER 1: Fire! And fire again!

NICOLA: [aside] TIME DEVIL, I'm going to get killed! [aside] Bullets were racing past my face, threatening to kill me.

BRITISH SOLDIER 2: Fire the cannons! Yes, let's turn that girl into exploding flesh!

BRITISH SOLDIER 1: Fire again!

BRITISH SOLDIER 2: Kill the traitor!

TIME DEVIL: Don't worry too much NICOLA, I bought the special Deluxe TimeBook Protection plan that offers 85% protection against violent death!

NICOLA: Only 85%?! What! That means, there's over a 1 in 10 chance I might be killed!

TIME DEVIL: You pesky pupils, always moaning about something, aren't you?

BRITISH SOLDIER 1: Another round of your best gunfire gentlemen please!

NICOLA: TIME DEVIL, you've got to get me out of here! Why are you going so close to the gunfire?

TIME DEVIL: Because I'd like to see whether you get killed or not!

NICOLA: You're insane!

TIME DEVIL: No, you're insane, you've betrayed your country and these loyal soldiers believe you must die!

NICOLA: The bullets are hitting you, but you're not getting hurt!

TIME DEVIL: That's because nothing can kill me except...

NICOLA: Except what?

TIME DEVIL: Now that would be telling, wouldn't it?

NICOLA: Argh! I'm hit.

TIME DEVIL: That must have been the 1 in 10 probability that you'd get hit?

NICOLA: Your protection plan is not protecting me! The bullets are real! I'm bleeding!

TIME DEVIL: Oh, it's only a scratch!

BRITISH SOLDIER 1: By Jove, we got her!

BRITISH SOLDIER 2: Now kill her! Blow her to bits!

BRITISH SOLDIER 1: Fire, fire, fire!!

NICOLA: TIME DEVIL, the bullets are hitting me! I'm going to die...

Learning Activities

Carry out Reciprocal Reading based on the scene you have read: explaining what has happened to each other, summing up how well you understood the passage, clarifying any problems you had with it, predicting what might happen next, or filling in the gaps in terms of feeling that there are things that are left out here; asking questions to help each other with summarizing, clarifying, predicting.

Predictions, hypothesizing and filling-in-the-gaps

Prediction 1: Were your predictions about the scene accurate? Did predicting what might happen motivate you to read the scene more than usual? If so, why?

Prediction 2: What might happen next in the script? Write down a summary in a spider-diagram of what you think might happen next in the rest of the script, then write it up as a short story.

Filling-in-the-gaps: What is left out in this scene? Do you think it is biased against the British? Does it present the British Empire in a negative light? Some people argue that the British Empire was a very positive force, others say it had a negative effect. You can start to explore the issues more here:

http://www.nationalarchives.gov.uk/education/empire/intro/default.htm

Hypothesizing: What do you think might have happened in India if India had achieved Independence in 1857, instead of 1948? What information might you need to get to help you "hypothesize" about this point?

Did discussing your predictions, filling-in-the-gaps and hypothesizing help you learn more?

Hold a debate about opium: once it was a legal drug but now it is illegal. Is this right?

Carry out Reciprocal Reading based on the scene you have read.

In your Learning Journal, devise a Spider Diagram of what has happened in the scene.

In your Learning Journal, write a prediction of what is going to happen next.

In your Learning Journal, note down what strategies are helping you improve your reading and why: re-reading passages you have skipped over or not concentrated upon, or found difficult; getting help and encouragement from other people in the group; thinking about things that interest you and relating them to the script; researching an aspect of the script in more detail.

Assessment point

To what extent were you Learning intentions met:
Learning intentions:
Grade yourself:

Learning intention	Unsatis-factory	Requires improve-ment	Good	Outstand-ing	Targets
I intend to learn more about making predictions and why they help you learn better.					
I intend to learn about "filling in the gaps" in our knowledge, and why this is important; spotting the "gaps" and trying to "fill them in"					
I intend to learn more about the different strategies for predicting, hypothesizing and filling in the gaps.					

What else did you learn? What do you think you should improve upon the most, and how might you do this in future lessons?

Independent study

- Find out more about opium and its role in history and society.
- Find out more about the Opium Wars which the British had with the Chinese and the Battle that Nicola finds herself in.
- These links could help you:
- https://en.wikipedia.org/wiki/Opium_Wars
- http://www.historytoday.com/julia-lovell/opium-wars-both-sides-now
- With your teachers & parents' permission, you could explore a very difficult topic: the Opium Trade. This is still a very controversial topic because our society has made the sale of opium illegal, except for medical purposes. Opium is often called 'heroin' or in slang 'smack' or 'junk'.
- This is an interesting article for a business magazine about the trade in drugs today:
- http://uk.businessinsider.com/how-drugs-travel-around-the-world-2015-2
- Why have so many writers written about opium? Find out about: Thomas De Quincy and Samuel Taylor Coleridge, the Velvet Underground's *Heroin*, Melvin Burgess's *Junk*.
- https://en.wikipedia.org/wiki/Opium_and_Romanticism
- https://www.bl.uk/romantics-and-victorians/articles/representations-of-drugs-in-19th-century-literature
- Continue reading another book/text related to the theme of time travel or a topic you are interested in connected with the script, noting down in your Learning Journal: what is happening in the book, what you like about it, what you think might happen next.
- Keep a list of useful vocabulary to learn and love.
- Find out about the National Maritime Museum by going on its website and skimming/scanning what is in the collection, why people might want to visit there, what interests you about the museum.
- Write about how you are finding the Reciprocal Reading so far, outlining your thoughts and feelings about how it went in the lesson. Discuss your thoughts and feelings with your friends, carers/parents and teacher.
- Watch some time-travel films, TV programmes and review them.

Lesson 7

Mindful reading meditation

Before starting your reading for the lesson, make sure you do a short mindfulness meditation to help develop your ability to set some clear reading intentions, to pay attention and adopt a positive attitude. Please see the section **Becoming a Mindful Reader** if you have forgotten how to do this.

Learning intentions: collaborating

Learning intentions	Learning Charm	How?	What?
I intend to learn more about why collaborating helps me learn.		By reading the lesson carefully, by following the instructions, by discussing with people in my group.	Discussion; notes; answering the set tasks.
I intend to learn about listening deeply to people, and to improve my ability to listen carefully to people.		By using questioning to "draw people" out more and by avoiding interrupting, but instead considering carefully what other people say.	Discussion; note-taking; answering the set tasks.

I intend to learn by helping other people: explaining points to them, asking them questions, praising them.		By reviewing how you best help people.	Discussion; note-taking; answering set tasks.

Are there any other things you intend to learn about? Please discuss and/or note them down...

Please read through your targets from last lesson and see if there is anything else you need to learn more about. Have a discussion about what you feel you need to improve with your reading and how you might improve your reading this lesson, e.g. by re-reading, by looking up difficult words, by having more of a positive attitude, to read with more expression, to think more deeply about what you are reading, to challenge yourself by reading more challenging material in your own time and bring that reading to the lesson to read when you finish the work or at the starts of lessons etc.

Learning script

ASSESSOR: How have you found collaborating with each other in groups so far? What has gone well and what has gone not so well?

MOTIVATOR: How do you feel about collaborating with other people to help them with your reading?

Learning to learn: how might you improve your collaborating in your group? How might you improve your listening to other people? How might you help people more?

TEACHER: in addition to the learning intentions set out above in the chart, see if you can think of some other intentions for this session which you can measure yourself against during the lesson. Be specific – like :

- •I intend to listen to everyone and not interrupt once.
- •I intend to make suggestions to help people with their Reciprocal Reading.
- •I intend to ask helpful questions which get people talking and thinking.
- •I intend to do my best to be imaginative with the predictions.

Are there any other things you intend to learn about? Please discuss and/or note them down...

Scene 7 Favor: Benin City: 1897

FAVOR: [aside] I was catapulted high over the Observatory and down into the museum, witnessing the exhibits in the Trade, Slavery exhibit. Horrors unimaginable. People packed in ships: their throats, their arms, their legs encased in chains. People being whipped and tortured, working the cotton fields, the sugar cane plantations in the fierce Caribbean heat. But also people in England protesting. Refusing to buy the sugar and clothes made from slave labour, protesting in the streets, protesting in parliament, and the law being changed so that slavery was no more. Just then I saw a black bird swooping down at me. Uh-oh!

TIME DEVIL (MISKI): Climb on my back Favor, I would like to take you to a proud kingdom in Africa.

FAVOR: Well, you don't get to hear much about great kingdoms in Africa, everywhere you go it's all about the great empires built by people from other continents. What part of Africa are we going to?

TIME DEVIL: I'm going to take you to one of the most ancient cities in the world, Benin City, in what is now Nigeria, but back in 1897 was the Kingdom of Benin, ruled by the mighty Oba, or king.

FAVOR: [aside] And so I climbed on the Time Devil's back and found myself flying with him straight at a big drum in a display case in the National Maritime Museum, passing through the glass, and into the drum itself, and then popping my head out of it, like a Jack-in-the-Box. I found myself in a big workshop where there were lots of musical instruments being made: drums, pipes, guitars. There were wood shavings everywhere and the smell of resin and glue.

OBA(TAI): Now Favor my son, I want you to make your Oba a wonderful drum that will be very loud when you bash it.

FAVOR: Hey, TIME DEVIL, where exactly am I?

The Time Devil: Teaching & Drama Script

TIME DEVIL: You, Favor are in the Oba's musical workshop making a drum for your great leader. A drum very similar to the one that is in the National Maritime Museum.

FAVOR: [aside] My head was poking through the hole of the drum; I realised I had to cover it with skin of some sort. I did this really badly but luckily a girl came over and showed me how to do it.

OBA'S DAUGHTER (MISKI): Papa, this boy doesn't know how to make a drum.

OBA: What's your name son?

FAVOR: FAVOR.

OBA'S DAUGHTER: Such a nice name! But he still doesn't know how to make drum!

OBA (TAI): That doesn't matter, you can show him. He's an outsider to the Kingdom of Benin, we can't expect him to know everything. The Gods in their merciful wisdom sent him here and that means we must treat him well. He's not like the Christian Missionaries we had to kill; they were bad men spreading their words about a false God like an infection through the land and trying to steal all my palm oil and ivory. No, Favor is not like them!

FAVOR: You had to kill some Christians?

OBA (TAI): Yes, my son. The Gods commanded me to, and I did that. Then I crucified them outside the walls of this great city, as a warning to anyone who crosses the mighty Oba. Follow me, I will show you my magnificent palace!

FAVOR: [aside] It was a great place, full of the most amazing statues of warriors brandishing all sorts of swords and weapons, wearing all kinds of great headdresses.

OBA'S DAUGHTER (MISKI): What's that noise, Papa?

FAVOR: It sounds like machine gun fire to me.

OBA'S DAUGHTER (MISKI): Papa, I can hear people screaming.

OBA (TAI): Do not worry, the Gods will protect us. The English said they would attack us for killing their missionaries, but they cannot defeat the power of the mighty Oba!

FAVOR: They can if they've got machine guns. Didn't the Time Devil say it was 1897? I'm not sure that the machine gun was created then. I thought it was developed for the First World War.

TIME DEVIL: A very simple, crude machine gun was invented in the late 1890s. It was the height of technology then.

FAVOR: And it would be enough to defeat people who only had spears and shotguns, wouldn't it?

TIME DEVIL: You can see for yourself!

FAVOR: [aside] Just then the doors of the Oba's Palace burst open and a bunch of sailors, sweating in heavy white Navy uniforms, rushed into the chamber, firing their guns and setting alight to everything they saw.

OBA (TAI): Stand back, you devils! You cannot defeat the mighty Oba!

FAVOR: [aside] The Oba's army rushed forward to protect their king. They were mighty warriors; I watched them in awe as they fought against the British Navy. There was much clashing of swords, spears being thrown, explosions everywhere, fire licking at the walls. The British Navy were not nearly as fit or expert at fighting as the warriors, who leapt around the room, thrusting and jabbing, wrestling and punching, jousting and throwing spears. But even though they were brilliant fighters they were no match for the Navy's guns and grenades, which popped and sizzled and exploded, until eventually the Navy had killed or injured most of them, and advanced upon the mighty Oba, who still stood proudly before his throne!

OBA: You cannot defeat me! I am the Oba! I command you to drop your weapons and surrender.

ADMIRAL RAWSON (CHARLIE): I am afraid my dear Oba, you have to drop your weapons or we will fire.

FAVOR: [aside] Just then, more warriors leapt out from the sides of the palace and fighting very bravely, grabbed the Oba and hurried him out of the palace.

OBA'S DAUGHTER (MISKI): My father has escaped! Oh wonderful!

FAVOR: As the Oba was escaped, the Navy fired more shots. I ducked out of the way just in time, but the Oba's daughter was hit as she tried to follow her father.

OBA'S DAUGHTER (TAI): I am hit, the devils have fired their poison at me. FAVOR, I am dying!

FAVOR: TIME DEVIL, this is terrible. The British Navy are stealing all the statues and burning the palace to the ground! Can't we do anything?

TIME DEVIL: Well, I do have something under my wing which might interest you.

FAVOR: Grenades! You've got some grenades. Give me them!

OBA'S DAUGHTER (MISKI): Oh Papa, I hurt but I am still alive to see this! FAVOR is fighting back! He's throwing these exploding balls at them, and they are running away!

FAVOR: Come on, grab some of these!

WARRIOR (CHARLIE): Yes, we will!

FAVOR: [aside] And I watched as the warriors came back, grabbing the grenades, which were far more effective than the grenades the English had. The British Navy yelled in fright.

ADMIRAL RAWSON ((CHARLIE): Men, retreat! Retreat! We need to get out of here!

FAVOR: Thank goodness, they've gone! We've won!

TIME DEVIL: You'd better use this TimeBook App First Aid Kit with the Oba's daughter, now.

FAVOR: [aside] I collected the First Aid Kit and stuck a magic plaster over the Oba's daughter's wound and then bandaged her up, and she came to life again.

OBA'S DAUGHTER (MISKI): Thank you, your magic equipment has healed me.

FAVOR: Just then the Oba reappeared, looking very pleased with himself.

OBA: Well done my son! I always knew I could count on you! We've defeated the British and stopped them from destroying my beautiful palace and city, and now this means I can continue to rule over my land!

FAVOR: TIME DEVIL, was that supposed to happen?

TIME DEVIL: Not really. In one universe, the British defeated the Kingdom of Benin, one of the great ancient African civilizations, burnt their city to the ground and took all their amazing statues. They are not in the National Maritime Museum but you can see many of them in the British Museum, in the basement, with a small plaque explaining what happened.

FAVOR: But what happens now that the Kingdom of Benin has defeated the British?

OBA: I rule over the land and get to kill more British people!

FAVOR: But I'm British, you shouldn't do that!

OBA: You're British! This is terrible. Men, execute this boy immediately.

WARRIOR 1: Yes Mighty Oba! Men, get your spears ready and take aim and throw them!

WARRIOR 2: Use your guns too! Fire at him!

FAVOR: TIME DEVIL, they're going to kill me!

TIME DEVIL: Funny, isn't it?

FAVOR: Argh! A spear has hit me in the arm. And I think I'm shot in the shoulder! Time Devil, I might die!

WARRIOR 1: Go in for the kill! Kill the terrible British boy!

WARRIOR 2: The traitor!

WARRIOR 1: Kill, kill, kill!

WARRIOR 2: Fire, fire, fire!

FAVOR: Argh! This is the worst thing that's ever happened to me! I think I'm going to die!

TIME DEVIL: This is what happens when you mess around with history!

Learning Activities

Carry out Reciprocal Reading based on the scene you have read: explaining what has happened to each other, summing up how well you understood the passage, clarifying any problems you had with it, predicting what might happen next, or filling in the gaps in terms of feeling that there are things that are left out here; asking questions to help each other with summarizing, clarifying, predicting.

Extension

Collaborating in groups, devise a radio report based on this scene, where you report on the defeat of the British Navy at the City of Benin.

Collaboration discussion

Using Reciprocal Teaching, discuss these points: How did the collaborating in groups go? How well are you helping each other? How good is your listening to each other as you read? How often do you praise each other and encourage each other to work harder? How much do you value collaborating together?

What strategies and attitudes helped you collaborate? How might you improve your collaborating in future?

Learning Journal Work

In your Learning Journal, devise a Spider Diagram of what has happened in the scene.

In your Learning Journal, write a prediction of what is going to happen next.

In your Learning Journal, note down what strategies are helping you improve your reading and why: re-reading passages you have skipped over or not concentrated upon, or found difficult; getting help and encouragement from other people in the group; thinking about things that interest you and relating them to the script; researching an aspect of the script in more detail.

Assessment point

To what extent were you Learning intentions met:
Learning intentions:
Grade yourself:

Learning intention	Unsatis-factory	Requires improve-ment	Good	Outstand-ing	Targets
I intend to learn more about why collaborating helps me learn.					
I intend to learn about listening deeply to people, and to improve my ability to listen carefully to people.					
I intend to learn by helping other people: explaining points to them, asking them questions, praising them.					

Independent study

- Find out about the Kingdom of Benin and the Oba; it's a fascinating story.
- **https://en.wikipedia.org/wiki/Benin_Expedition_of_1897**
- **https://en.wikipedia.org/wiki/Ovonramwen**
- Visit the British Museum and see the Benin Bronzes, the statues stolen from Benin City by the British Navy.
- Continue reading another book/text related to a theme in this script, e.g. time travel, noting down in your Learning Journal: what is happening in the book, what you like about it, what you think might happen next.
- Keep a list of useful vocabulary to learn and love.
- Find out about the National Maritime Museum by going on its website and skimming/scanning what is in the collection, why people might want to visit there, what interests you about the museum.
- Write about how you are finding the Reciprocal Reading so far, outlining your thoughts and feelings about how it went in the lesson. Discuss your thoughts and feelings with your friends, carers/parents and TEACHER.
- Watch some time-travel films, TV programmes and review them.
- If your carers etc. up a blog for your group, and note down your thoughts/feelings about Reciprocal Reading.

Lesson 8

Mindful reading meditation

Before starting your reading for the lesson, make sure you do a short mindfulness meditation to help develop your ability to set some clear reading intentions, to pay attention and adopt a positive attitude. Please see the section **Becoming a Mindful Reader** if you have forgotten how to do this.

Learning intentions: learning to learn

Learning Intentions	How?	What?	Learning Charm
I intend to learn more about the things that best motivate me to learn.	By thinking carefully about what motivates me to learn; by discussing this seriously.	Discussion; notes; answering the set tasks.	
I intend to learn more the ways in which all the topics covered can help me learn.	By looking back at the strategies already covered in the script: summarizing, predicting, skimming and scanning, questioning, collaborating.	Discussion; note-taking; answering the set tasks.	
I intend to learn more about what I think and feel about my learning.	By questioning myself about my learning and getting people to question me in detail.	Discussion; note-taking; answering set tasks.	

Please read through your targets from last lesson and see if there is anything else you need to learn more about. Have a discussion about what you feel you need to improve with your reading and how you might improve your reading this lesson, e.g. by re-reading, by looking up difficult words, by having more of a positive attitude, to read with more expression, to think more deeply about what you are reading, to challenge yourself by reading more challenging material in your own time and bring that reading to the lesson to read when you finish the work or at the starts of lessons etc.

Learning script

LEARNING TO LEARN CHIEF: What attitudes help you learn? What feelings help you learn? What feelings do not help you learn?

MOTIVATOR: If you are feeling angry or depressed in a lesson, how does this help you learn? What might you do in this situation?

ASSESSOR: How can you assess your own learning? What are the benefits of assessing your learning?

Are there any other things you intend to learn about? Please discuss and/or note them down...

Scene 8 Miski: female soldier, German ship, 1914-18, WWI warship, Jutland

MISKI: [aside] The Time Devil threw me down the hill in Greenwich Park and I found myself flying above the trees and straight into the ship in the bottle, which, as soon as I had landed on it, began to rattle, rumble and ratchet out of the bottle. I grabbed the ship's wheel and steered it through the opening glass doors of the museum, guiding it towards the exhibit that interested me most: Jutland 1916: World War One's Greatest Sea Battle. As soon as I'd entered the dark cavern of the exhibit, I found out that my ship was bobbing up and down on a stormy sea. A big black bird flew above my head, squawking at me, and then it came and settled on my shoulder.

TIME DEVIL (NICOLA): That's a very nice ship you've got there, Miski! But it's not going to be much use against them!

MISKI: [aside] I looked and saw lots of huge grey war ships pointing their cannons at me. These weren't old fashioned cannons, but were seriously nasty looking weapons. I am going to get killed! The cannon balls tore apart my frail little ship within minutes and I found myself clinging onto the wreckage, trying to keep my head above water. The water was cold, very cold. Time Devil, help me! I'm drowning.

TIME DEVIL (NICOLA): Sorry, I don't like to get my feathers wet! But never mind, there's a ship heading your way.

MISKI: [aside] I looked and saw one approaching. There was a slight problem though, it wasn't a British ship, it had the German cross on it!

GERMAN SAILOR (CHARLIE): Achtung!

MISKI: I don't understand German, Time Devil! Can't you help with that?

TIME DEVIL (NICOLA): OK, I'll download TimeBook Translate into your brain; I did it for everyone else, but never got around to you!

GERMAN SAILOR (CHARLIE): Young girl, come here! Catch this rope!

MISKI: Thank you! [aside] The German sailor pulled me onto the ship, and wrapped me into a blanket.

GERMAN SAILOR (CHARLIE): What are you doing here? We're in the middle of the worst sea battle of the war and you decide to go out in a wooden boat. Are you crazy? We thought you were the enemy so we fired!

MISKI: I'm sorry, but I just didn't quite realize what I was getting myself in for, I just thought it was all a bit of a joke.

GERMAN SAILOR 2 (FAVOR): Bring her down below and give her a nice of cup of tea to warm up.

MISKI: [aside] And so I went down below on the ship, and sat shivering by the stove, admiring the enormous golden kettle that they had on the hob. I have never seen such a huge kettle!

GERMAN SAILOR 1 (CHARLIE): We must have a big one to keep all the men happy with their cups of tea. It's the happiest moment in a sailor's life; to have a nice warming cup of tea.

GERMAN SAILOR 2 (FAVOR): Oh dear, what is that? It's the siren again. The British are attacking!

GERMAN SAILOR 1 (CHARLIE): They are close, very close! We will almost certainly die if we don't do something soon. And the Captain is telling us that we have been shooting at our own ships. It's getting too dark to see anything!

MISKI: [aside] Just at that moment, my phone buzzed. It was TAI. Hey, TAI where are you?

TAI: I'm in the National Maritime Museum looking for you! You wouldn't believe it, but I had the strangest dream! I dreamt that I was at the Battle of Trafalgar and I saved Lord Nelson's life and changed the course of British History! Where are you?

MISKI: I'm in the Battle of Jutland.

TAI: Yeah, cool, I'll come and find you!

MISKI: No, you don't understand, I am in the real Battle of Jutland, with some German sailors here having a cup of tea.

TAI: Do you mean it's real? Send me a picture!

MISKI: So I did, taking a picture of myself next to the copper kettle.

TAI: Whoa, how did you do that? I'm standing right next to that kettle!

MISKI: TAI, you don't get it, I'm in this smelly, dirty German ship; I am not joking. I'll send you another picture. It stinks in here, and I feel genuinely sea-sick and I'm wet through from falling into the sea, this is real, real, real.

TAI: I wouldn't believe you except that something similar happened to me in what I thought was a dream, but I realize now I really did feel the cold of that sea too. It's freezing cold, isn't it?

MISKI: It's terrible! I got the shock of my life!

TAI: And smelly too! People didn't wash back then, did they?

MISKI: This ship smells of disinfectant, sweat and stuff I don't want to tell you about. I'm nearly gagging!

TAI: So you are really there, aren't you? Crazy, or what!

MISKI: Hey, do you know what you could do me a favour, could you text me some photos of the maps of the battle, TAI? Maybe they would help me get out of this mess! I could maybe figure out a way of getting off this ship!

TAI: Sure. I'm sending them right now…

GERMAN SAILOR (CHARLIE): Are you speaking to someone who knows where all the ships are? How is that possible?

MISKI: [aside] Just at that moment, the photos of the positions of the ships at Jutland in the exhibition came through on my phone; before I knew where I was, the German soldier had grabbed my phone out of my hand! Hey, give me that back!

GERMAN SAILOR (CHARLIE): What is this thing? It's a sort of metal book! Goodness me, these pictures, they are maps of where the ships are during this battle, am I right? I am calling the CAPTAIN, this is amazing. We know where the British ships are: thanks to this metal book, we can tell their exact positions!

MISKI: Oh no! Won't the British be sitting ducks now?

GERMAN CAPTAIN (FAVOR): Quite right, I have the positions of the ships. Men, battle stations, we're going to win the Battle of Jutland!

MISKI: Uh-oh, I've really messed up!

GERMAN CAPTAIN: Come on boys! Fire away!

MISKI: [aside] I rushed out on deck, and saw that with my phone in his hand, the CAPTAIN was aiming his guns into the darkness, and then guiding the ship. Suddenly, I saw one ship burst into flames, there was lots of firing, and another ship exploded. All around me the sky was filled with explosions, fire, smoke, men screaming the most terrible screams you've heard in your life. What have I done? I want my phone back!

GERMAN CAPTAIN: You are not permitted to have this metal map; it is confiscated!

MISKI: Give it to me!

TIME DEVIL: It's fun, this battle, isn't it? Rather nice to see the Germans on the winning side for once, isn't it?

MISKI: You are evil, Time Devil. This was not supposed to happen. The Germans weren't supposed to win this battle! Look, there's another British ship destroyed. I rush over to the German

CAPTAIN, and finally manage to get the phone out of his hands.

GERMAN CAPTAIN: You are an enemy to the German people! Sailors! Kill this girl immediately!

GERMAN SAILOR 1: Kill her! Men, get your guns and take aim!

GERMAN SAILOR 2: Fire at her!

GERMAN SAILOR 1: Kill the enemy of the Kaiser!

GERMAN SAILOR 2: Kill the enemy of the German people!

GERMAN SAILOR 1: Fire your revolvers, rifles and guns at her.

GERMAN SAILOR 2: Give her all the firepower you've got!

MISKI: TIME DEVIL, stop this! I'm going to die!

TIME DEVIL: I paid for the Deluxe TimeBook app protection package: 85% protective against violent death and disease when time-travelling. Good, heh?

MISKI: Not a 100%?

TIME DEVIL: Yes, I've received some complaints about that! But look on the bright side, it does bring the excitement of genuine risk into this jolly time-travelling game, doesn't it?

MISKI: But I might die!

TIME DEVIL: Yes, there is always that; and this weaponry makes it highly likely you will. But would you really want to live in a world where the Germans won the First World War? Most historians think it would have led to the Germans being the single greatest power on earth, dictating to all people's their harsh terms and conditions! Everyone would want to kill you I think! Better to die now!

MISKI: I'm hit! The pain is unbearable! I'm going to die!

TIME DEVIL: Oh, come on, death will be a merciful release!

MISKI: [aside] With that I was falling down, down, down into a terrible and scary darkness, screaming for my life, feeling the pain of the bullets sizzle and sear my body!

Learning Activities

Carry out Reciprocal Reading based on the scene you have read: explaining what has happened to each other, summing up how well you understood the passage, clarifying any problems you had with it, predicting what might happen next, or filling in the gaps in terms of feeling that there are things that are left out here; asking questions to help each other with summarizing, clarifying, predicting.

Learning to Learn: review of what helps you learn

What strategies helped you learn during the reading? Think about:
- Your learning intentions; did have clear learning intentions help you learn better?
- Your attitude towards your learning; did having a positive attitude help you learn better?
- Your attention; did paying attention carefully to the reading help you better learn?
- Re-reading
- Asking questions to help you work out what was happening
- Being positive about the reading and seeing the good aspects to the reading
- Discussing your thoughts and ideas with other people
- Predicting what happens next
- Summarising the passage either by saying a summary
- Summarising the passage by writing down a summary

Notes

In your Learning Journal, devise a Spider Diagram of what has happened in the scene.

In your Learning Journal, write a prediction of what is going to happen next.

In your Learning Journal, note down what strategies are helping you improve your reading and why: re-reading passages you have skipped over or not concentrated upon, or found difficult; getting help and encouragement from other people in the group; thinking about things that interest you and relating them to the script; researching an aspect of the script in more detail.

Assessment point

To what extent were you Learning intentions met:
Learning intentions:
Grade yourself:

Learning intention	Unsatis-factory	Requires improve-ment	Good	Outstand-ing	Targets
I intend to learn more about the things that best motivate me to learn.					
I intend to learn more the ways in which all the topics covered can help me learn.					
I intend to learn more about what I think and feel about my learning.					

Independent study

- Continue reading another book/text related to the theme of time travel, noting down in your Learning Journal: what is happening in the book, what you like about it, what you think might happen next.
- Keep a list of useful vocabulary to learn and love.
- Find out about the National Maritime Museum by going on its website and skimming/scanning what is in the collection, why people might want to visit there, what interests you about the museum.
- Write about how you are finding the Reciprocal Reading so far, outlining your thoughts and feelings about how it went in the lesson. Discuss your thoughts and feelings with your friends, carers/parents and TEACHER.
- Watch some time-travel films, TV programmes and review them.
- If your carers etc. up a blog for your group, and note down your thoughts/feelings about Reciprocal Reading.

Lesson 9

Mindful reading meditation

Before starting your reading for the lesson, make sure you do a short mindfulness meditation to help develop your ability to set some clear reading intentions, to pay attention and adopt a positive attitude. Please see the section **Becoming a Mindful Reader** if you have forgotten how to do this.

Learning intentions: summarizing part II

To learn more about how to summarize; to learn how to get the overall gist of a passage; to learn how to use a range of strategies to summarize a passage.

Learning intentions	Learning Charm	How?	What?
I intend to learn more about how to summarize passages.		By reading the lesson carefully, by following the instructions, by observing in my group the people who are good at summarizing and learning from them.	By discussing my ideas in my group in a helpful, collaborative way.
I intend to learn more about how to work out the overall gist or meaning of a passage and/or the script.		By thinking hard about whether I understand the passage for myself.	By writing a summary.
I intend to learn more about the different strategies for summarizing a passage or the whole script.		By reading the script about this point, and discussing it with members of my group.	By having a go at different ways of doing summaries, e.g. written/spoken, spider-diagrams, bullet points etc.

Are there any other things you intend to learn about? Please discuss and/or note them down…

Scene 9 The Greenwich Meridian: the Final Confrontation

ALL SIX ACTORS TOGETHER: Hey! I thought I was going to die!

FAVOR: You too?

CHARLIE: I thought I was dead Favor.

MISKI: But you're alive! And I am too!

NICOLA: And so I am I!

TAI: Yes, it hurt a lot!

PADRAIG: Life hurts generally. We don't live in a nice world!

FAVOR: But now it feels as if we are floating in space!

CHARLIE: I feel like I'm not floating, but falling!

TAI: Through emptiness.

NICOLA: Falling through nothing.

FAVOR: Blackness all around.

PADRAIG: I can see the darkness! The darkness is visible!

MISKI: And the darkness is in my head. A horrible, evil darkness!

CHARLIE: And I'm hurt! I had soldiers in red coats firing their muskets at me! And I saw the Prince of Wales bleeding to death in front of me! It was a nightmare!

TAI: I'm hurt too! Admiral Nelson ordered me to be killed because I saved his life and turned him into a nobody! And his men were mean! It was a terrible nightmare!

PADRAIG: I was hit as well! Rocks and boulders from outer space were bashing into me! My chest and legs were on fire! It was terrible!

NICOLA: No, you guys have no idea what pain is! I had the British Indian army attacking me just because I wanted the Indians to gain their freedom! It was a nightmare to end all nightmares!

FAVOR: Hey, if you're talking pain, you have no idea what kind of pain I was in! I had the mightiest warriors the earth has ever seen stick their spears into me! And all because I saved their Oba's life, and wanted to stop him killing the British! After all, I am British! It was seriously horrible. If you took all the nightmares that everyone ever dreamt, then this would be the most frightening!

MISKI: Look, I was properly shot; I was more less killed! Shot to pieces by the German navy, and I think even more awful is the knowledge that I made the world a much, much darker place by helping the Germans win the First World War! It's all TAI's fault! She shouldn't have texted me those photos of the Battle of Jutland! I am just eaten up with guilt; just to think that I have caused so much suffering and pain!

CHARLIE: And so I am!

MISKI: And so I am! How can I live with myself?

TAI: This has been the worst thing that's ever happened to me!

CHARLIE: But hey guys, I know we're falling through space and things feel really bad, but I think we should try and calm down and think.

NICOLA: Yes, Charlie is right, let's calm down and figure out a few things. What did you do again, Miski? I still can't get my heard around it. It feels like all of us went to specific times and changed history.

MISKI: I think just I changed the outcome of the First World War! The Germans won it! How crazy is that?

NICOLA: What did you do Tai?

TAI: I think I changed British history forever by healing Nelson at the Battle of Trafalgar.

MISKI: But you were also in the Battle of Jutland exhibit in the National Maritime Museum, how did that happen?

TAI: Yeah, that's the strange thing, after Nelson nearly killed me, I found myself back in the actual room where the picture of the Battle of Trafalgar is in the National Maritime Museum, and realised that I sort of fell into it, and it became real. So, not wanting that to happen to me again, I ran next door into the Battle of Jutland exhibit, that's when you contacted me.

And almost immediately after I sent those pictures to you, I found myself falling through space like this, until I met you guys, feeling the wounds which Nelson's men had given me again.

MISKI: That is completely mad!

FAVOR: What happened to you, Charlie?

CHARLIE: I think I helped the Dutch become a world superpower. And you Nicola? What did you do?

NICOLA: I think I helped the Chinese win their 2nd Opium war against the British and the Indians defeat the British in 1857. How about you, Favor, what did you do? We all need to figure out what happened to us.

FAVOR: I think I helped an African nation become great again. I believe I saved an ancient beautiful culture from ruin, but did I get thanked for it, oh my goodness, no!

PADRAIG: And I think I have a big decision to make!

MISKI: But hang on a minute, what would happen if the Germans won WW1?

TAI: I know I thought at first only bad things would happen, but now, being away from that horrible Time Devil and being with my friends, it does make me think more positively. Maybe there would have been no Nazi Party, and no Holocaust, and no nuclear bombs!

CHARLIE: What would have happened if the Dutch had had a great empire and not the English?

MISKI: Maybe they would have helped other nations be friendly to each and stopped lots of wars?

NICOLA: What would have happened to India if it had been free to choose its own destiny a hundred years before it got independence?

CHARLIE: Maybe it would have avoided becoming so poor and having so many of its people suffer from malnutrition, disease and poor education.

FAVOR: What would have happened if African culture had been treasured and celebrated instead of being mocked, demonised and destroyed?

MISKI: Maybe, Africa and the other nations on earth would be much happier and people would want to dance, sing, and be free in their lives!

CHARLIE: But let's think about this before we hit the earth and die. The Time Devil made us do those things, and then feel bad about them, but maybe, thinking it through, we might have done some good?

MISKI: Yes, you never quite know what effect an action will have, do you?

TAI: And if you have a kind heart and do things for the right reason, maybe that will make good and not bad things happen?

FAVOR: Or maybe not, I helped the Oba, but then he said he wanted to kill me. My good intentions led to bad things happening.

TAI: Yes, that's true with me too. When Admiral Nelson realised that he wouldn't be remembered as a hero, he ordered his men to kill me!

NICOLA: But you don't know that for certain. Maybe that was the Time Devil messing with your mind!

CHARLIE: Yes, I heard that Nelson was a good guy. He didn't kill innocent people! Maybe he was an evil double created by the Time Devil to mess with your mind?

TAI: But the shots they fired at me were real!

MISKI: Yes, the guns were real!

CHARLIE: That gunpowder filled the air with its smoke.

FAVOR: Those spears really hurt!

NICOLA: Yes, the weapons were real.

FAVOR: But we all seem to be OK now.

PADRAIG: Maybe that's because we've been flung into a time before all that happened?

NICOLA: What do you mean?

PADRAIG: Well, haven't you noticed that we are falling, and falling, and falling, and we never seem to touch the ground?

MISKI: Yes, but I can see a planet below us.

TAI: It looks like earth to me. All those clouds and blue sea. It's beautiful!

CHARLIE: It won't be beautiful if we fall slap bang into the middle of it.

NICOLA: Look, we're falling through the atmosphere, through the clouds, through the blue sky.

FAVOR: I can see America, Africa, Australia, the North and South Pole. It's amazing. This is much better than sky diving!

PADRAIG: Yes, but have you noticed that we don't have parachutes?

ALL SIX ACTORS TOGETHER: AAAAAH! We're going to die!

CHARLIE: But hang on a minute, we seem to have stopped; we're about 50 feet off the ground now.

MISKI: And flying like Superman! Yay! We are saved! I knew the TIME DEVIL was good really. It was all just a bad dream!

PADRAIG: Look, I can see the Time Devil is hovering over the Greenwich Meridian, near the National Maritime Museum.

TAI: Greenwich Park looks beautiful in the summery light!

NICOLA: And the National Maritime Museum and Queen's House look lovely!

CHARLIE: I think we're nearly home guys. All we need to do now is to fly off to Deptford!

FAVOR: But I don't seem to be able to move! I am frozen up here above the Greenwich Meridian, the line that divides east and west, the centre of all the time zones.

MISKI: And we stuck in the air right above it!

TAI: Not able to move! Uh oh!

CHARLIE: And can you see how time is changing?

TAI: Yeah, it's cool. It's like staring into a gigantic 3-D cinema screen.

NICOLA: Yeah, it is like we are watching time go backwards.

MISKI: All the mistakes and tragedies and terrible things of history are being undone.

FAVOR: The slaughter of the nations is being reversed, people are not killing each other.

CHARLIE: Bullets and bombs are flying out of people's bodies.

NICOLA: And people's bodies are being healed.

TAI: And everything is being healed.

CHARLIE: There are no more wars, and fighting.

MISKI: Jealousy and envy.

FAVOR: Hatred and anger.

CHARLIE: And time is going backwards, right to the beginning of everything.

NICOLA: And it's happening so fast! I can't believe it, in the blink of an eye, we seem to be at the beginning of the earth again.

FAVOR: Look, there's no life on it at all.

TAI: Wow! That was quick!

TIME DEVIL: So, guys, we come to the crunch point, the moment we have all been waiting for!

CHARLIE: What?

MISKI: Yes, what is the Time Devil talking about?

NICOLA: Just when you think everything is going to be OK, they aren't!

TAI: Yes, that's a familiar feeling!

PADRAIG: I know what it is. This is the moment I have been dreading. I must make my decision.

FAVOR: What was it?

PADRAIG: Whether to guide that comet you can see right there into the earth, thereby starting life.

TIME DEVIL: And once you do that, all of the things that your friends have done will come true! After all, they did a lot of good, didn't they?

MISKI: I'm not sure about that.

FAVOR: Yes, I'm inclined to agree.

NICOLA: But you've got to do it Padraig, otherwise none of us would exist. And we're only taking the Time Devil's word that the things we did will alter history.

CHARLIE: Yes, and you could argue that we've changed things so that history turns out better.

PADRAIG: But does it? Will it? Maybe the Dutch will do just as many bad things as the British did? You saw what happened when you tried to do the right thing!

CHARLIE: Oh, come on, that is being a bit 'Dutchist', isn't it? I've got Dutch heritage, and I am a nice guy!

NICOLA: And I'm English, and that doesn't make me a horrible colonial murderer!

FAVOR: But I know what PADRAIG means, I mean, there is no absolute certainty that just because Nelson lived that he would make Britain a more caring place.

TAI: He would make Emma Hamilton much happier. She died a lonely old woman without him. I suppose there's that. And the English wouldn't have made such a big fuss about it; maybe it would have been good for us not to have such an important national hero.

MISKI: I suppose Padraig has a point. Human nature is human nature, and there are good and bad people in all nations, and places.

TIME DEVIL: And I think Padraig should have learnt by now, that whatever you do, it always turns out bad. All of you altered history, but did you make things turn out better? Well, I'm afraid to say you didn't! Charlie just replaced the violent British Empire with a violent Dutch Empire, Tai turned Nelson into a forgotten nobody, Tai's intervention in China and India led to the slaughter of thousands of people in terrible wars of independence, Favor helped an African dictator kill more English people and then get defeated by the English anyway, and Miski helped the Germans become the world super power. You see guys, whichever way you look at things, bad things always happen! Death, disease, mass murder, violence are just facts of life on earth!

TAI: Don't listen to him PADRAIG, he's messing with your mind! Like he did with all of us! We must have hope things will turn out well; we need to trust in life.

CHARLIE: And we're all friends, aren't we? Maybe we should all join hands and jump on that comet and make sure it gives life to earth.

TAI: Yeah, make it a collaborative decision. It's not a decision PADRAIG can make alone.

The Time Devil: Teaching & Drama Script

MISKI: Yes, we should all take responsibility for what happens!

FAVOR: Yes, we are all in this thing together!

TIME DEVIL: No, you can't do that! You don't understand, it's Padraig's decision to make, that's the way I designed the game!

NICOLA: And now we're taking charge of the game together TIME DEVIL! You can't control all six of us!

MISKI: We've got too much brain power between us! We're a group now, not just isolated individuals!

PADRAIG: Thanks guys, you've made me think that perhaps there is hope!

TIME DEVIL: You horrible people! That wasn't what I wanted! I think it's time I sorted out all out! Devils, kill them!

CHARLIE: Suddenly lots of horrible spiky, squirmy, snaky devils appeared in the sky and dived towards us.

ALL SIX ACTORS TOGETHER: AAAH! We're being attacked!

DEVIL 1 (MISKI): You get NICOLA and impale her with your red-hot spear!

DEVIL 2 (CHARLIE): You get Miski and machine gun her to death with your special Devil gun!

DEVIL 3 (FAVOR): You get Charlie and hack him to death with the sharpest knives that were ever made!

DEVIL 4 (TAI): You get FAVOR with your axe and lop off his head, that'll stop him talking!

DEVIL 5 (PADRAIG): You get TAI and disembowel her with cutlass!

DEVIL 6 (NICOLA): You get Padraig and drive a spike through his eyes!

MISKI: Come on guys, let's join hands together and see if we can defeat them.

CHARLIE: There's no way we can beat them physically; they're weapons are too powerful!

FAVOR: What are we going to do? Fight?

TAI: We're going to die!

NICOLA: Well, maybe we are, but maybe we need to die in the right way? I think we should remember that meditation exercise we did in school yesterday – or a few billion years in the future -- and shut our eyes, take a deep breath, and think kind thoughts.

FAVOR: What good is that going to do?

MISKI: It might help us die a nicer death?

PADRAIG: All we have really is this moment now, isn't it? And since we can't beat them, we need to think about good things, not bad things…

CHARLIE: Yes, let's shut our eyes and wish those devils well; they must be quite messed up in their heads to be so violent for no reason whatsoever.

TIME DEVIL: No, no, no! You're supposed to fight them.

NICOLA: Come on, let's shut our eyes and wish ourselves well, and everyone else in the universe well. Let's wish kindness and love on everyone!

MISKI: Nice deep breath in, follow the breath through our throats, down into the chest and into the stomachs, and say to ourselves, with each in-breath I am calming!

CHARLIE: And with each out breath I am smiling!

PADRAIG: Hold hands and breath in, breath out.

FAVOR: And wish everyone well in our minds.

PADRAIG: Smile kindness upon everything and everyone!

TIME DEVIL: No, no, no!

PADRAIG: Even though my eyes are closed, I can feel the Time Devil shrinking.

TAI: Yes, with my eyes shut, concentrating upon my breath going in and out, in and out, I can feel the Time Devil becoming an ordinary bird!

CHARLIE: And with my eyes shut I can feel that we're back on that comet and it's is heading straight for earth!

MISKI: Let's keep the meditation up guys, with eyes shut, we breathe in, we breathe out. We say to ourselves like they did in the meditation at school: "May we be happy, may we be kind to ourselves, may we have ease of being!"

NICOLA: Like FAVOR said, we're in this together!

FAVOR: And it's strange but meditating like this on the comet that made life on earth I can feel the power of all of us thinking kind thoughts together.

PADRAIG: And smiling at the thought that we are giving life a chance!

TIME DEVIL: You can't do this! You don't realize what you're doing! You're going to make the earth into a nice place where people are kind to each other! This is bad, very bad! There will be no more wars, divisions, fights, prejudices! Humans, animals and nature will live together in harmony. There will be no disastrous climate change, nuclear weapons and terrorism! There will be no more devils like me! All the fun will be sucked out of life! ARGHH!!

PADRAIG: That stuff is only fun for devils like you!

TIME DEVIL: I'm disappearing, withering, fading away; I am no longer needed or wanted! You're turning me into a Time Angel, not a Devil! ARGHH!

NICOLA: Don't open your eyes! That's what he wants! Let's continue thinking kind thoughts! We shaping our world with our minds!

CHARLIE: And we could feel a light filling all of our heads and bodies, a light of compassion and kindness.

ALL SIX ACTORS TOGETHER: There was a huge explosion and life began on earth!

PADRAIG: We opened our eyes and found ourselves in a very familiar scene. Fordham Park. Eight thirty in the morning. Outside Deptford Green school.

MISKI: Hey, where are we?

FAVOR: What's that noise?

CHARLIE: It's the school bell.

NICOLA: We're going to be late!

TAI: What's the first lesson?

PADRAIG: We have got that meditation exercise, remember? You know, to help us stop being anxious all the time…

MISKI: Oh yeah, it might be nice and relaxing. De-stress us and stop us worrying about exams…

CHARLIE: Hey, look there is a big black bird in the sky. Does it remind you of anything?

MISKI: Yeah, it does.

FAVOR: It makes me think of life on earth for some reason.

NICOLA: And the strangeness of being alive.

TAI: It is makes me think that being here right now just outside Deptford Green school is really amazing. Just being with my friends, learning things together, it's actually quite great! We're alive and we're smiling at each other!

PADRAIG: Hey, do you think the Time Devil was telling the truth? Do you think we've changed things so that there are no wars or conflict?

MISKI: We'll have to go to school and find out, I guess!

CHARLIE: Hey, good idea!

End of the Time Devil script

Learning Activities

Carry out Reciprocal Reading based on the scene you have read: explaining what has happened to each other, summing up how well you understood the passage, clarifying any problems you had with it, predicting what might happen next, or filling in the gaps in terms of feeling that there are things that are left out here; asking questions to help each other with summarizing, clarifying, predicting.

Choose the summary activity which will best help you learn more about the scene or if you like have a go at summarizing the whole script:

- Having read the scene, now shut your eyes and replay the scene in your head. What parts leap out at you? Open your eyes and write down the key things that have happened in the passage. How did you find shutting your eyes and taking a "breathing space" to think about the passage?

- Use a highlighter to highlight the important lines in the scene. Using these highlighted bits, write a summary of the scene in your own words. How did you find this approach which is to "edit" down the passage to the important lines/words?
- Ask a specific question of the passage, which could be "What does Padraig experience in this scene?" and answer it. How did you find this approach to summarising; i.e. asking a specific question and answering it.
- Visualise the scene, and draw pictures/symbols of the important parts of it; it doesn't matter how good you are at drawing, it's the way you summarise the scene it that is important. How did you find this approach?
- Spider diagram the scene. How did you find this approach?
- Compare and contrast the scene with what has happened before, showing how what happens to Padraig is similar and different to what happened to Tai and Charlie. How did you find this "compare and contrast" approach to summarising?

Further exercises

In your Learning Journal, devise a Spider Diagram of what has happened in the scene.

In your Learning Journal, note down what strategies are helping you improve your reading and why: re-reading passages you have skipped over or not concentrated upon, or found difficult; getting help and encouragement from other people in the group; thinking about things that interest you and relating them to the script; researching an aspect of the script in more detail.

Assessment point

To what extent were your Learning intentions met:
Learning intentions:
Grade yourself:

Learning intention	Unsatisfactory	Requires improvement	Good	Outstanding	Targets
I intend to learn more about how to summarise passages.					
I intend to learn more about how to work out the overall gist or meaning of a passage and/or the script.					
I intend to learn more about the different strategies for summarising a passage or the whole script.					

Independent study

Utopias and Dystopias

Find out more about dystopias (worlds that have gone wrong): **https://en.wikipedia.org/wiki/Dystopia**
Find out more about utopias: (perfect worlds): **https://en.wikipedia.org/wiki/Utopia**
Do some Reciprocal Teaching/Reading based upon the above Wikipedia pages, following up the references and links that interest you. Watch relevant films/plays; read relevant books/plays/poetry; listen to songs/poems etc. Devise a booklet called "My Perfect World" where you

outline what a perfect world might look like. Or do a booklet on "Worlds Gone Wrong", and write some poems, stories, plays etc which describe and dramatize worlds that have gone wrong.

The 'Time-Travel' project

Find out more about the Greenwich Meridian.

Find out about the writers who have written poems/stories about the Greenwich Meridian. Why has it fascinated writers over the ages?

Write your own story/poem set by the Greenwich Meridian.

Continue reading another book/text related to the theme of time travel, noting down in your Learning Journal: what is happening in the book, what you like about it, what you think might happen next.

Keep a list of useful vocabulary to learn and love.

Find out about the National Maritime Museum by going on its website and skimming/scanning what is in the collection, why people might want to visit there, what interests you about the museum.

Write about how you are finding the Reciprocal Reading so far, outlining your thoughts and feelings about how it went in the lesson. Discuss your thoughts and feelings with your friends, carers/parents and TEACHER.

Watch some time-travel films, TV programmes and review them.

If your carers etc. up a blog for your group, and note down your thoughts/feelings about Reciprocal Reading.

Lesson 10

Learning intentions: motivating yourself

Learning Intentions	Learning Charm	How?	What?
I intend to learn more about the things that best motivate me to learn.		By thinking carefully about what motivates me to learn; by discussing this seriously.	Discussion; notes; answering the set tasks.
I intend to learn more the ways in which all the topics covered can help me learn.		By looking back at the strategies already covered in the script: summarizing, predicting, skimming and scanning, questioning, collaborating.	Discussion; note-taking; answering the set tasks.
I intend to learn more about what I think and feel about my learning.		By questioning myself about my learning and getting people to question me in detail.	Discussion; note-taking; answering set tasks.

Please read through your targets from your previous lessons and see if there is anything else you need to learn more about. Have a discussion about what you feel you need to improve with your reading and how you might improve your reading this lesson, e.g. by re-reading, by looking up difficult words, by having more of a positive attitude, to read with more expression, to think more deeply about what you are reading, to challenge yourself by reading more challenging material in your own time and bring that reading to the lesson to read when you finish the work or at the starts of lessons etc.

Learning script

TEACHER: What have you enjoyed most about reading the script?
ASSESSOR: What have you found the most difficult and why?
MOTIVATOR: What motivates you to read and why?
QUESTIONER: What questions help you learn more?
SUMMARIZER: What summarizing techniques help you understand a passage?
LEARNING TO LEARN CHIEF: What learning to learn strategies help you learn generally?

Final Assessment point

To what extent were you Learning intentions met for the whole unit of work?
Learning intentions:
Grade yourself:

Learning intention	Unsatisfactory	Requires improvement	Good	Outstanding	Targets

Motivation

In general, when you read texts in school, how motivated and confident do you feel when you read them now that you have done this unit:

4	3	2	1
Not motivated at all	A little	Quite motivated	Very motivated

In general, when you read texts outside school (social media etc), how motivated and confident do you feel when you read them now that you have done this unit:

4	3	2	1
Not motivated at all	A little	Quite motivated	Very motivated

Skimming and scanning

In general, when you read texts in school, how good do you believe you are at skimming (quickly looking through a text and working out what it means) and scanning (quickly looking through a text to find a specific piece of information) through texts and working out what might be happening in them now that you have done this unit? Please tick:

4	3	2	1
Not very good	OK	Good	Outstanding

In general, when you read texts outside school, how good do you believe you are at skimming and scanning through texts and working out what might be happening in them? Please tick:

4	3	2	1
Not very good	OK	Good	Outstanding

Please write a comment about how you good you feel you are at skimming and scanning:

Summarising

In general, when you read texts in school, how good do you believe you are summarizing the content of what you read now that you have done this unit? Please tick:

4	3	2	1
Not very good	OK	Good	Outstanding

In general, when you read texts outside school (which can include social media/articles you like etc), how good do you believe you are summarizing the content of what you read now that you have done this unit?

4	3	2	1
Not very good	OK	Good	Outstanding

In general, when you read texts in school, how good do you believe you are summarizing your understanding of what you read now that you have done this unit? Please tick:

4	3	2	1
Not very good	OK	Good	Outstanding

Please write a comment about how you good you feel you are at summarizing now that you have done this unit:

Clarifying and questioning

In general, when you read texts in school, how good do you feel about asking questions which might help you work out what a difficult text means now that you have done this unit? Please tick:

4	3	2	1
Not very good	OK	Good	Outstanding

In general, when you read texts outside school (which can include social media/articles you like etc), how good do you think you are at asking questions which might help you work out what a difficult text means now that you have done this unit?

4	3	2	1
Not very good	OK	Good	Outstanding

Please write a comment about how you good you feel you are at clarifying (working out what difficult texts mean by yourself) and questioning now that you have done this unit:

Predicting

In general, when you read texts in school, how effective are you at predicting what might happen next now that you have done this unit? Please tick:

4	3	2	1
Not very good	OK	Good	Outstanding

In general, when you read texts outside school (which can include social media/articles you like etc), how effective do you think you are at predicting what might happen next now that you have done this unit?

4	3	2	1
Not very good	OK	Good	Outstanding

Please write a comment about how you good you feel you are at making predictions of what might happen next in a text now that you have done this unit:

Collaborating

In general, how good do you think you are at collaborating with other students in school so that you might improve your learning about a topic now that you have done this unit? Please tick:

4	3	2	1
Not very good	OK	Good	Outstanding

In general, how good do you think you are at collaborating with other students outside school so that you might improve your learning about a topic now that you have done this unit? Please tick:

4	3	2	1
Not very good	OK	Good	Outstanding

Please write a comment about how you good you feel you are at collaborating now that you have done this unit:

Learning to learn

In general, how good do you think you are at working out what helps you learn more independently now that you have done this unit:

4	3	2	1
Not very good	OK	Good	Outstanding

Please write a comment about how you might developed your learning to learn knowledge and skills during this unit:

Suggestions

Any suggestions about how we might improve this script to help people improve their reading skills?

Independent and collaborative study based on the whole script

- Film or record some scenes of the play.
- Devise a chat show based on the play.
- Make a documentary about the play and film it. See the one from last year based on 'My Dreams, My World': **https://www.youtube.com/watch?v=Lr8bQI597Nw**
- Make a film based on an edited version of the play. You can see the one done last year based on 'My Dreams, My World': **https://www.youtube.com/watch?v=YDRNRu2Hjxo**
- Read more plays and write your own TIME DEVIL script, about your friends cast back in time in the Deptford area. Do some research about the area and get them to meet real people, e.g. Sir Francis Drake, Samuel Pepys, John Evelyn.
- Hold a debate about whether the script presents the history in a fair and balanced light. Does it present the British too negatively? Is it too jokey in tone considering these are real events that have happened?
- Continue reading another book/text related to the theme of time travel, noting down in your Learning Journal: what is happening in the book, what you like about it, what you think might happen next.
- Keep a list of useful vocabulary to learn and love.

- Find out about the National Maritime Museum by going on its website and skimming/scanning what is in the collection, why people might want to visit there, what interests you about the museum.
- Write about how you are finding the Reciprocal Reading so far, outlining your thoughts and feelings about how it went in the lesson. Discuss your thoughts and feelings with your friends, carers/parents and teacher.
- Watch some time-travel films, TV programmes and review them.
- If your carers etc. up a blog for your group, and note down your thoughts/feelings about Reciprocal Reading.
- Write a review of this script and, after carefully editing of it, post it on a site such as Amazon where the book is for sale, or another relevant blog/website. Here are some guidelines about how to write a good book review: **http://www.booktrust.org.uk/books/teenagers/writing-tips/tips-for-writing-book-reviews/**

The key questions for Reciprocal Reading

First part of the reciprocal reading cycle
What is this scene about? What is happening in it? How might I best summarize my overall understanding of the passage: do I have a unsatisfactory, satisfactory, good or outstanding understanding of the passage? **(Summarizing)**

Second part of the reciprocal reading cycle
Are there any difficult bits we don't understand? Is anything not very clear? If so, can other people in the group help us understand the scene better? **(Clarifying)**

Third part of the reciprocal reading cycle
Does anyone have any questions to ask about the passage? Do you have any questions about how you might improve your understanding of the passage? **(Questioning)**

Fourth part of the reciprocal reading cycle
What does everyone think might happen next? Is there anything that is NOT said in the scene/passage that we think might be important to consider? **(Predicting/hypothesizing)**

Fifth part of the reciprocal reading cycle
How well are we reading? What could we do to improve our reading? **(Assessing/Evaluating/learning to learn)**

About the author

Francis Gilbert is a Lecturer in Education at Goldsmiths, University of London, teaching on the PGCE Secondary English programme and the MA in Children's Literature with Professor Michael Rosen. Previously, he worked for a quarter of a century in various English state schools teaching English and Media Studies to 11-18 years. He has also moonlighted as a journalist, novelist and social commentator both in the UK and international media. He is the author of *Teacher On The Run, Yob Nation, Parent Power, Working The System -- How To Get The Very Best State Education for Your Child*, and a novel about school, *The Last Day Of Term*. His first book, *I'm A Teacher, Get Me Out Of Here* was a big hit, becoming a bestseller and being serialised on Radio 4. In his role as an English teacher, he has taught many classic texts over the years and has developed a great many resources to assist readers with understanding, appreciating and responding to them both analytically and creatively. This led him to set up his own small publishing company FGI Publishing (fgipublishing.com) which has published his study guides as well as a number of books by other authors, including Roger Titcombe's *Learning Matters* and Tim Cadman's *The Changes*.

He is the co-founder, with Melissa Benn and Fiona Millar, of The Local Schools Network, **www.localschoolsnetwork.org.uk**, a blog that celebrates non-selective state schools, and also has his own website, **www.francisgilbert.co.uk** and a Mumsnet blog, **www.talesbehindtheclassroomdoor.co.uk**.

He has appeared numerous times on radio and TV, including Newsnight, the Today Programme, Woman's Hour and the Russell Brand Show. In June 2015, he was awarded a PhD in Creative Writing and Education by the University of London.

Printed in Great Britain
by Amazon